In Love with a Convict

**Lock Down Publications
Presents
In Love with a Convict
A Novel by *CA$H***

In Love With a Convict

Lock Down Publications
P.O. Box 1482
Pine Lake, Ga 30072-1482

Copyright 2012 by CA$H

First Edition December 2012
Printed in the United States of America

Lock Down Publications
Book interior design by: **Shawn Walker**
Graphic Design by: **Dynasty's Cover Me**

Stay Connected with Us!

Text **LOCKDOWN** to 22828 to stay up-to-date with new releases, sneak peaks, contests and more…

Thank you!

Submission Guideline.

Submit the first three chapters of your completed manuscript to ldpsubmissions@gmail.com, subject line: Your book's title. The manuscript must be in a .doc file and sent as an attachment. Document should be in Times New Roman, double spaced and in size 12 font. Also, provide your synopsis and full contact information. If sending multiple submissions, they must each be in a separate email.

Have a story but no way to send it electronically? You can still submit to LDP/Ca$h Presents. Send in the first three chapters, written or typed, of your completed manuscript to:

LDP: Submissions Dept
Po Box 1482
Pine Lake, Ga 30072

DO NOT send original manuscript. Must be a duplicate.

Provide your synopsis and a cover letter containing your full contact information.

Thanks for considering LDP and Ca$h Presents.

Ca$h

Chapter 1
Prince

"Yo, mayne, you gotta come see the new lieutenant! That bitch cuter than a muthafucka and thick as hell, too," exclaimed Dushay, as he burst into the cell bouncing up and down like he had never seen a pretty woman before.

The entire prison population was talking about Lieutenant Nicole Wright, who had transferred to Georgia State Prison two weeks ago from the prison across the street. I hadn't seen her yet, but muthafucka's swore she was a beautiful redbone with ass for days. Now, that could've been true, but I wasn't hyped. Georgia dudes was forever exaggerating shit, ya heard me. Besides, I wasn't no groupie-type nigga.

"Mayne, hurry up! She down on the first tier right now!" Dushay excitedly continued. His Memphis, Tennessee accent made *man* come out *mayne*.

"If you've seen one dime piece you've seen 'em all, woady." I cautioned him with my New Orleans flava. Then I continued writing my dirty ass baby mama, Solange, a kick rocks letter.

"Nawl, mayne this female is buck; you ain't ever seen 'nan' as fly as this one," Dushay persisted.

I shook my head. "Bruh, you becoming just like these Georgia clowns. Get off her bra strap, ya heard me. 'Cause a dime ain't worth shit if she won't hold a man down."

Those sentiments echoed what I was saying to Solange in the letter. The way she was shittin' on a nigga had me salty with all pretty hos. Fuck Lieutenant Nicole Wright, let all those other fools drool over her, I wasn't about to be one of her fans. Besides, what was they sweating her for? More than likely, she wasn't gon' fuck with an inmate and jeopardize her job.

Dushay saw that I wasn't on that type of time so he pushed on, and I finished writing the missive to Solange. After I showered, I kicked back and listened to Rick Ross' CD titled, *Teflon Don* while flipping through my photo album. Those pics took me down memory lane. *I was stunting hard when I was on the bricks.*

I wasn't but twenty-seven years old, but I had plenty bands out there. I didn't slang yams because the crack game was way too grimey. Instead, I dealt exclusive weed and sold x-pills by the hundreds. Most of the big-time hustlers in ATL copped Kush or beans from me. I wasn't rich, but I was livin' good, ya heard me.

I drove a black on black Escalade and a silver metallic Mercedes CLK. Both were sitting on chrome and plushed out with the luxuries inside. My gear was always tight, and my jewelry game was stupid sick. Every time I pulled up on the block those ATL girls went crazy. They simply loved New Orleans niggas— whoa nah.

I wasn't on them like that though. I had cuffed Solange soon after moving here, so I was good. All she had to do was stay looking good, take care of Asia, our five year old daughter, and be my comfort when I came home out of the streets. I can't even front; I was sprung on her sexy red ass. Even after I found out that before we hooked up she had been nothin' but neighborhood pussy.

"Ya past don't matter, ya heard me. Those niggas just didn't know how to appreciate a diamond in the rough," I told her one day when her history came out through the mouth of one of her so-called friends.

I would be lying if I said that stories of Solange letting different block huggers run up in her didn't faze me, but I manned up and gave lil' mama a clean slate. Gave her every luxury and convenience imaginable, and never once played her with no other chick.

Now that I was on lock and she was showing her true colors, I regretted being real with her bird ass. It's true, you can't turn a ho into a housewife, ya heard me.

On every picture in the album she was rockin' designer labels, expensive jewels, and a smile that attested to how well I treated her. On several of the pics she stood in front of the lipstick cherry-red

Dodge Charger that I had bought her punk ass. I bristled inside as the pain of her betrayal bubbled up in my chest.

Scowling, I snapped the album closed and laid back on my hard, state-issued pillow with my hands folded behind my head. I tried to push thoughts of Solange out of my mind as I contemplated a move that I was putting together to receive two pounds of loud and fifty beans. A cool CO named Johnson was fuckin' with me the long way. I had to get my paper right in order to hire a top flight attorney to appeal my conviction. Fuck lying around serving a life sentence.

I shouldn't have had to grind up attorney fees because I had left two hundred bands out there. My partna, Jamal, had stuck me for $60,000 that I loaned him. Solange ended up getting robbed for the rest. I was still hotter than fish grease over that! Had she followed my instructions and not procrastinated, the stash wouldn't have been at her house.

It was all good though. *Muthafuckas gonna pay!* I fumed inside as I got up and walked out on the tier. To my surprise, down below, Lieutenant Wright was talking to the floor officer. I knew it had to be her by the many descriptions I had received of her. Niggas hadn't lied; her beauty made a me stare. Her long black hair was in a silky ponytail that reached midway down her back. Her complexion was the same as Solange's. I could tell even through the drab work uniform that she had a body that could turn a preacher against his congregation.

She looked up and our eyes held each other's for an unusually long moment. *You cute, bitch, but so what?* I was thinking. The tier was crowded with inmates gawking at her. I broke our eye contact and went back inside my cell. I had had enough of pretty broads!

I flopped back down on my bunk and tried not to think about Lieutenant Nicole Wright. She reminded me way too much of Solange. And that was an absolute turn off.

Ca$h

Chapter 2
Solange

It was early August, and the Atlanta sun was peeking in through the slight openings in the vertical blinds of my bedroom window. I turned over on my side in my Cali King-sized bed, rubbing my shaved and satiated kitty kat against the nigga's thigh who was lying next to me. He stirred, but didn't awake. This wild monkey between my legs had an effect on men that put them to sleep with their thumbs in their mouths.

The clock on the nightstand read 12 o'clock noon, straight up and down. Ughhh! I had not intended on sleeping so late, but I hadn't gotten in until 4:00 A.M. Last night, I had gone out to the new night-club out in Buckhead and partied like a rock star! I could still picture the screwed faces of the jealous hos when I climbed on top of the bar in VIP. I stripped down to my red thong for all the caked up niggaz in the nightclub to see what a bitch was working with. My bare titties showed no signs of childbirth, and my tummy was flat. My ass is a baller's dream, and we won't even discuss this phat coochie because trust, it's indescribable. Bitches were hating, hurling insults when my little impromptu strip dance ended.

Fuck y'all! I thought as I sauntered back to the booth, garments and niggas money in hand.

"Bitch, you're bold." My bestie Tash laughed. "Cover up your titties!"

"Don't hate, it's really not a good look," I replied flippantly as I licked my thumb and counted the money that I had collected popping pussy. Six hundred and thirty dollars for dancing two songs. Had a bitch contemplating becoming a stripper.

I had so many niggas on my thong I could hardly breathe. I was *that* bitch, and every ho up in the club could only get sloppy seconds. Good thing Asia was spending the night with my mother because all of that attention had started my clit to jumping. Plenty niggas had

11

wanted to take me home and dick me down. I was in bad need of some dick, but I hadn't wanted to get with just any nigga and chance choosing one that couldn't bring me to an orgasm. So I chose to ride out with the one lying next to me because we had messed around in the past, and his dick game was the bomb.com.

In the wee hours of the morning, he had long dicked me so good I damn near forgot my name. The muthafucka had licked my coochie so wonderfully that I was considering commissioning someone to make a bronze bust of his head and putting it on the mantle in my living room like a trophy. But now that I had gotten three super intense orgasms, it was time for him to get out.

I shook him. "Jamal, wake up. It's time for you to go."

"What time is it?" he grumbled.

"Time to go!" I repeated myself.

He sat up in bed and wiped sleep from his eyes. "Dayum, shawdy, you get the dick then put a brotha out? Can't you at least bring me breakfast in bed?"

"You sound stupid." I clucked my tongue against the roof of my mouth. "You can go in the kitchen and fix yourself a bowl of cereal, but I don't do room service." I made it clear.

"Yeah, you on that bullshit." He huffed swinging his legs over the side of the bed and standing up to his full six-one height. I took in his physique; he had a nice chest that tapered down to his little four pack of stomach muscles. Eight inches of thick meat and big ol' balls hung between his muscled legs.

My eyes traveled up. Jamal rocked dreads that hung down to his shoulders, and he was kinda cute. If I would have been strictly a cum freak, I would've been so gone over him. That was not gonna happen because his hustle game was backwards. Every time he got his bank-roll right, he wound up losing it shooting dice or playing high stakes poker. His up and down hustle was not attractive at all. In truth, I felt somewhat bad about kicking it with Jamal anyway because he was my baby daddy's 'so called' friend.

My heart still belonged to Prince, although I'm sure my actions contradicted that. I mean, I truly loved him, but I had a very high sexual nature. Prince could do nothing from prison to satisfy it so a bitch had to get it elsewhere. Why was I fucking his partna out of all people? I questioned myself.

Call it convenient dick if you will.

Of course, such treachery came with a whole lot of guilt. I hadn't been to visit Prince in six months because every time I went to see him he would ask me who I am seeing. "Nobody. I'm waiting on you, Daddy," I'd lie, but I knew that he could see straight through me.

The hurt in his eyes would be so visible. It was as if his pain were words written on pages of an open book. I would feel some kind of way about lying to him, but I would rather die than admit to sleeping with Jamal. To Prince, that would be unforgivable. *Loyalty Over Er'thang* was tatted across his chest. Prince had really looked out for me when he was on the streets hustlin'. So for me to sleep with any other nigga, let alone his man, would be the kiss of death to our relationship in his eyes. I saw it much differently. With the new laws in effect, a life sentence meant that he would serve a minimum of thirty years in prison! What woman can keep the pussy locked that long?

"Shorty, fix me something to eat," Jamal's voice interrupted my thoughts.

Irritated I replied, "This is not IHOP, dude. You better act like you know."

"Damn. Why you always talkin' breezy to a nigga?" he asked, stretching then retrieving his clothes from the floor by the bed.

"Look, Jamal, I'm not in the mood to go there with you this morning. I need to get my day started, and this is not how I want to do it."

"Yeah, whatever," he mumbled.

I went and hopped in the shower, washing away as much of my infidelities as possible. Jamal stepped into the shower with me, trying to get another piece. I put my hand against his chest and lightly pushed him away. "I have things to do." I rejected him. I hurried and washed, then left him in the shower with his dick in his hand.

Twenty minutes later, he was dressed and came into the kitchen where I was. I had gone outside to check for the mail. Now I was at the kitchen table sorting it out.

"That bet' not be no letter from that nigga. If it is , we 'bout to have some problems," Jamal threatened, standing over my shoulder sweating the letter in my hand.

"Excuse you?" I said with a tsk.

"You heard me."

"Yeah, I heard you, but you ain't talking about nothing. You don't pay no bills up in here!"

Whap! His hand came out of nowhere and connected with my face.

Oh, hell to the nawl! I know this nigga didn't just slap me! I was stunned.

I tossed the letter down, sprang up from the table, and dashed over the counter. "I got something for your monkey ass!" I spat, whirling around, now holding a butcher knife. "You just hit the wrong bitch!" I charged after his ass, intent on gutting that muthafucka'. "Don't 'nan' nigga put his hands on Miss Shirley's daughter!" I hissed, quickly closing the distance between us.

Jamal's eyes bulged, then his coward ass took off running out the back door. I rushed out behind him screaming, "That's right, run you little bitch!"

I skidded on the heels of my feet as I turned the corner of my house. I spotted him clad in his blue Ralph Lauren T-shirt, and Levi jeans that sagged down revealing the top of his blue boxers. The bottom of his blue low-top Converses were kicking up dust. Behind him my 36 C's were bouncing up and down, threatening to pop out of my wife beater. I was barefoot in boy shorts that had crawled all the way up my ass. Booty cheeks flashed for all of my neighbors to see.

Glancing next door, I saw my elderly neighbor, Mr. Sam, in his rocker on his porch. Besides him, no one else was out. I had much respect for my elders, but today he was gonna witness a bitch act a fool!

Jamal hurried inside of his black '64 Chevy Impala that was parked in the driveway behind my car. His bitch ass was locking the door as I ran up to the driver's side breathing heavily. "Get your bitch ass out and hit me now, muthafucka!" I dared him.

"Fuck you, maggot-ass bitch!"

"Oh, I got your maggot bitch." I huffed quickly looking around for something to smash his window in with. I dropped the knife and picked up one of the grapefruit sized white boulders that decorated the edge of the front lawn. I hurled it through the window of the driver's door, with all of my might.

The whole window exploded in a spray of shattered glass.

"Bitch, I'ma kick your ass!" Jamal growled.

By the time he unlocked the door and hopped out of the car, I had retrieved the butcher knife. "Put your hands on me, mutha-fucka', and I swear your mama will have to bury that ass!" My chest heaved up and down.

I saw the punk come out of him as he stood there looking like he was trying to decide if he could win against a half crazy hood bitch with a big ass knife in her hand. "Don't get caught slippin', Solange," he warned. Then he got back in his whip, backed out of the driveway, and peeled off.

I took a few seconds to calm myself down before walking over to Mr. Sam's and apologizing for literally showing my butt in front of him.

"Young lady," he said. "It's none of my business what you do, or who you do it with—all I'ma say is that you never had to go through things like that when Prince was here. I read in the paper what they say that boy did, and maybe he was guilty of what he was convicted of. I tell you this: you'll never hear me say one bad thing about that boy because from what I saw he treated you and that pretty lil' girl of y'all's like queens. A man that loves and respects his woman and child can't be too bad."

"That's true, Mr. Sam," I agreed.

"And don't you turn your back on him, he deserves better."

"Yes sir. And, again, I apologize for what you saw."

As I made my way back home, Mr. Sam's words rang in my ear and tore at my heart. He was so right about Prince. Every nigga that I had fucked with before him had cheated, lied, and abused me, but Prince had been my knight in shining armor.

By the time I returned to the kitchen and sat down at the table to read Prince's letter, the tears had begun to pour. *Baby, I miss and need you so much,* I said inside.

My hand shook as I tore open his letter. What I needed most was to read that he still loved me, and that we could get through this together. I needed his encouragement because without that I was not strong enough to ride the way he needed me to. All hopes of encouragement was shattered from the first words he'd written.

Solange it's over between you and me and ain't no way to reverse it. I'm done holding my breath every weekend hoping you'll show up. When I think about how you have switched up on me since I caught this bid, I realize that you never loved me in the first place. I thought you was a rider, but you was just a hitchhiker lookin' for a free ride. What I took for a hidden gem was really a muthafuckin' germ! Your beauty hid your ugly ass heart. This bid revealed the truth about who and what you are. I may be down right now but like yeast I'll rise. This is the last time I'll ever write you. Take care of my daughter. One.

16

Tears flowed down my face. I crumpled up the letter and rested my head on the table. I felt so bad about abandoning Prince. I decided that I didn't want to lose him regardless of his circumstances. *I gotta go visit him,* I said to myself.

Ca$h

Chapter 3
Prince

"**I**nmate Prince Myers report to the control booth. You have a visit," sounded over the intercom in the cell block.

"Fuck!" I sighed with agitation. Now was not the ideal time. My move had just come through and me, Dushay, and Stack were in my cell bagging up oz's and fifty sacks.

"Go ahead and get ready for your visit, mayne, me and Stack can finish this," suggested Dushay.

"No, woady. I'ma put it up until I get back. I fuck wit' y'all, but I can't stand no losses. I'm grinding for my freedom, ya heard me."

"It's whatever wit' me, fam," said Stack, a young hitta from Southeast Atlanta who was known in prison for pushin' that knife. I fucked wit' homie because he was real. He was a Gangster Disciple, but he wasn't on the bullshit like most dudes behind bars who were affiliated.

Dushay said, "Mayne, you trippin'. How you gon' take a loss by leaving the shit with us? We your dawgs. You know we gon' handle business the way it's supposed to be handled."

"I feel you, but leaving my shit in the hands of others is what got my stomach touching my back now." I scooped my shit up and stashed it inside the heater vent in my cell. I saw Dushay's face twist in a scowl, as if he had a problem with my decision. "Get out of your feelings, bruh." I checked him.

He nodded his head. "Whatever, fam."

"I'ma get up wit' y'all when I get back," I said. We dapped each other and they bounced.

I took a quick shower then came back to my cell and lotioned my tall, lean frame. I put on my icy white and crisp khakis. I ran a brush across my spiraling waves, stepped into my fresh white Air Force Ones, and put on my platinum cross. I grabbed the eye drop bottle out of my wall locker and dabbed on a little Prada cologne. I checked my reflection in the mirror above the sink in my cell. Hair spinning, baby face, thick brows, coal black eyes, and swagged up. *Whoa nah!* I was looking like I was about to hit the club.

"Never let 'em see you at less than your best," I said to my reflection.

I didn't have to guess who was visiting me because Solange and Asia's names were the only people on my visitation list. The little family I had back in New Orleans wasn't hittin' on shit, the streets had raised me. That's why it was crushing me for Solange to switch up. I had put my all into her and my seed.

I was tempted to decline the visit, but that would've been foul. Asia hadn't done anything to deserve that. My princess was crazy about me, and she made a nigga's eyes light up. Fuck Solange's trifling ass. I would just fall up in the V.I. and chill with my seed.

As soon as I stepped in the visitation room and spotted Solange by herself, my forehead wrinkled. She stood up and flashed me a smile as I approached the assigned table. "Hey, baby daddy," she had the nerve to say like shit was all good.

I breathed in and out. *Smiling like she ain't violated a nigga!* It was hard to contain the beast within. Asia ran up from behind me, hugging my leg. "Whoa nah." I turned around and flashed her a sincere smile and bent down and picked her up.

"Hey, baby girl, I didn't see you when I walked in."

"I was at the water fountain."

"Gimme a kiss, Pretty One," I said.

Asia's arms went around my neck and she gave me a big kiss, ending it with, "Umm."

"Your kisses are so delicious," I said.

"Yours are too, Daddy," she sweetly replied.

I stared at her for a second. Her light brown complexion was a mixture of my dark chocolate skin tone and Solange's redbone color. Her sandy-red hair, light brown eyes, and dimpled smile was all her mother's. It pained me to think that my beautiful daughter could possibly grow up to have a heart as cold as her mom's. *Nah, I wouldn't let that happen,* I promised myself.

I sat my daughter down and looked at her no-good mama. Solange said nothing. She sat back down at the table wearing an expression that I interpreted to mean she was waiting for me to speak back. I sat across from her. My eyes were slits as I took in her appearance. Her hair flowed past her shoulders; two long bangs hung down her face. Her pouty lips and the phony smile that she flashed me was a sign of deception.

I tried not to stare at the contours of her body in the white BCBG jumpsuit, because now that bangin' body was gettin' pleased by the next nigga.

The sweet scent of her perfume usually made my dick swell, but now that shit was rank from so much dishonesty. My thoughts went back to when I was out in the free world. I had often put Solange's wants over my *needs*. All that had mattered was seeing shawdy happy, straight up. A nigga took penitentiary chances to give her the best. Looking at her pretty muthafuckin' ass now, I felt played. I wanted to smash her face in. I wanted to hurl some real foul shit at her to make her feel my pain. But how do you hurt a heartless bitch? I asked myself.

"You look good. How you been, baby daddy?" she asked.

"I'm good, ya heard me," I replied dryly. The tone of my voice was two tones deeper than usual.

"Um, I got your letter last Saturday. I decided to come and see you since it sounded like you were becoming bitter toward me." She reached across the table and stroked my arm. I knocked her grimey ass hand away.

"We ain't rockin' like dat. Stop frontin' like shit still cool and just keep doing you."

Solange rolled her eyes. I turned my attention to Asia. "Baby girl, are you doing good in school?" I inquired.

"Yes, Daddy. Next month I'll be out for Labor Day. Will you be home by then?"

Her innocence broke my heart.

"I don't think so, sweetheart." It was as close to the truth as I could muster.

"Daddy, why you gotta stay here?"

"I'll explain it all when you get older," I answered.

"Asia, stop asking your daddy so many questions," Solange cut in.

"Don't fuss at her." I mean mugged her.

"She ask too many question. All day long—Why? Why? Why…"

"I do not," Asia disagreed.

Before I knew it Solange had popped her in the mouth. "Don't you backtalk me!" she gritted.

Asia wailed like Solange had knocked her teeth out. I hugged my baby and growled under my breath to Solange, "Hit her again and I'ma punch you in your shit."

"And when you do Jesus gon' weep," she shot back.

I ignored her slick remark because if I went there, shit was gonna go from zero to a hundred in one second flat.

"You okay, baby girl?" I asked Asia, rubbing her back and wiping her tears away with my shirt.

She nodded her head up and down, sniffling. Close to forty-five minutes passed without another word being spoken between me and her mama. Solange had her arms folded across her chest, and I wasn't studying her trife ass. I happened to look up once and caught her mean-mugging me, she would have to blink before I would. I eye grilled her with eyes only a demon could possess, and she quickly looked off.

Finally she asked, "You want something out of the vending machines?" She picked up the plastic bag of quarters that she had brought along.

"I'm good."

"Humph! I could've stayed my red ass at home in the bed instead of driving three and a half hours for this bullshit," she retorted rolling her neck. "You have a real nasty attitude."

"I ain't got no attitude', I just don't fuck with you or your kind no more."

Solange sucked her teeth. "What the hell you mean by *my kind*? What fucking kind are you classifying me as, Prince?"

I looked dead in those deceitful eyes of hers that used to hold my heart captive, but not anymore. "You don't want me to answer that," I released with a voice full of venom.

"Oh, yes I do," she insisted, so I spit it to her raw.

"You'sa nothin' ass broad who'll only get with a nigga to get you where your sorry ass tryna go. You ain't gonna work for shit; you fuck niggas for handouts."

Solange gasped first. Then she hissed, "You black ass muthafucka! Who are you to judge somebody?"

"I'll call a spade a spade."

"I hate you!" she hurled.

"The feeling is mutual, ya feel me?"

"I hope your ungrateful ass die in here."

"Oh, yeah? What about Jamal? You hope he lives forever so he can keep running up in you, huh?" I tossed back at her.

Asia's head was swinging back and forth like a yo-yo. My last statement caused Solange to choke on her own tongue.

"You're speechless now, ain't you? Asia go get a drink of water, baby," I ordered my daughter with my eyes focused on her mama.

Asia got up and did as I said. I waited until she was out of earshot before I gave it to Solange's shady ass. "Bitch, you're nothin' to me now. Out of all the niggas you could've fucked, and I'm sure you've fucked many, you busted your legs open for a nigga that I ran with. Only a dumb ho gets down like that. If it wasn't for Asia I would have your punk ass murked, fa sho'."

She waved me off. "Boy, you sound silly. Ain't nobody fucked Jamal. I don't know who you're getting your information from, but you need to double check it before you bring that mess to me. For real, you sound retarded."

"You talk fly to Jamal like this? What about all those niggas at the nightclub that you stripped naked for and popped your pussy? You out there doing ho shit, disrespecting my name in the streets. Trick, don't come down here to see me again." My lip quivered with fury.

Tears ran down Solange's face like raindrops during a storm, but they didn't mean shit to me.

Asia came skipping back. "Mama, why you crying?" she asked staring up into Solange's face.

Solange ignored the question. She sprang up out of her seat and snatched Asia by the arm. "Come on, we're leaving. Your daddy has pissed me the fuck off!" Her voice had grown so loud it attracted everyone's attention in the room. "What the fuck are y'all looking at me for? Mind y'all own damn business! Nosey bastards!" she snapped after seeing how people were turning around staring from their seats.

No one said anything.

"I'm not ready to go!" cried Asia.

"Bring your ass on!" seethed Solange. She seized her by the arm and swooped her up like a limp dishrag.

"I love you, baby," I called to my daughter as she was being dragged out by the arm, kicking and crying.

As they exited the room, I could do nothing but ask myself why had I fucked with Solange's grimy ass in the first place.

Chapter 4
Solange

Leaving the prison, I was a mess. Tears streamed down my face and the taste of snot was in the back of my mouth. I was hurt and furious. I didn't know who had busted me out to Prince, but I had a good idea.

I waited until Asia fell asleep on the long ride home then I hit up Tash.

"Hey, bitch. How was your visit?" she cheerfully asked.

"Terrible."

"Why? What happened?" She sounded concerned. That set my blood boiling. If there was one thing I couldn't stand, it was a back-stabbing bitch.

"Trick, don't play dumb! You've been telling Prince all my business," I accused while driving. I reached over and lowered the music on my radio so I could really hear what the bitch had to say.

"Gurl, have you lost your fucking mind?" She snapped.

"No, but I'ma lose this size seven up your ass when I catch you."

"Solange, what are you talking about?" Tash continued her charade.

"Bitch, don't act slow. How the fuck did Prince know that I've been fucking with Jamal if you didn't tell him?"

"You're fucking Jamal?" She burst out laughing. "Dang, ho. I didn't know that. Eww!"

I thought about it for a minute, Tash was telling the truth. I hadn't ever told her about me and Jamal. But the bitch could've told on me about other things. "Ok, well how did Prince find out what I did at the club last weekend?" I questioned her.

"How would I know, Solange? I don't know how to contact Prince. Besides, you're my bestie. I wouldn't cross you like that."

"Mmm hmmm," I replied. I did not trust bitches. "Don't let me find out you're lying, heffa."

"What—eva. Anyway, now that you put it out there, is Jamal's dick as good as bitches claim?"

"Better." We laughed.

"How big is it?" she asked.

"I don't know, bitch. I haven't measured it, but it got a hook in it that hits my spot," I shamelessly revealed. Shit, Tash couldn't judge me, her pussy should've been looser than diarrhea the way she gave her goodies out.

"Can he eat pussy?" she pried, sounding like she was interested in more than the answer.

"Why don't you stick yours in his face and find out. Trust, I don't give a damn. I'm through with his lame ass anyway."

"Why? What did he do?"

"His broke ass had the nerve you try to check a bitch." I told her about the altercation.

"Gurl, you stay in some drama." She giggled.

"No more than you do, ho," I reminded her before she could get brand new on a bitch.

In the middle of our conversion, my phone chirped. "Chile, hold on a minute. Let me answer my other line." I clicked over without looking at the caller ID. "Hello."

"Sup, shawdy? You still mad at me?"

"Nigga, fuck you! And don't call my phone no gotdamn more!" I clicked back to Tash. "Can you believe that nigga had the nerve to call me? He got me twisted."

"Who Prince?"

I cocked my head to the side and curled my lip up. "No, bitch, Jamal."

"What he say?"

"Uh…moving right along," I sarcastically replied. 'Cause I wasn't in the mood to be jaw jabbin' about his lame ass.

"Any who. Don't nobody want Jamal. So who do you think Prince has watching you?"

"I don't know. Could be anyone. You know he has a lot of home-boys." Just then I saw flashing lights in my rearview mirror. "Oh, shit! I gotta go." I hung up and pulled over on the shoulder of the highway. A few seconds later, a tall, brown skinned highway patrol-man came up to the driver's door.

I rolled the window down, smiled, and batted my naturally long eyelashes at him.

"Good afternoon, Officer. Is there a problem?" I made it sound like, *would you like for me to suck your dick?* After that he was putty in my hands.

Thirty minutes later, I drove away with a number that I would never use locked in my phone. While Asia slept the entire drive back home, I listened to Frank Ocean's CD. *'Thinking About You'* trav-eled through my speakers as I tried to come up with a plan to win Prince back.

Ca$h

Chapter 5
Prince

When I left visitation, my face was stone. Solange was making my bid much harder than it had to be with all the deceitful bullshit. I knew she was lying about that nigga Jamal.

My anger was so thick that it threatened to choke me. I regretted cutting the visit with Asia short, but I had no regrets about what I'd said to Solange. The bitch deserved every foul word I'd thrown at her.

All Solange had to do was keep it one hunnid, and I would've tried to understand her position. At the end of the day, I would've bent over backwards to provide Asia with the family I never had. Now that was impossible because I would have to be a fuck boy to allow Solange to shit on me and take her back.

Ain't no muthafuckin' way! I vowed as I walked back to my housing unit, still steaming inside.

The first thing that I did when I returned to my cell was retrieve the weed from the stash spot. Immediately, I saw that the spot had been tampered with, and the weed looked to be a few ounces short.

"Oh, hell the fuck nawl!" I said to myself. Stack and Dushay are the only ones that could've stolen it. "Y'all niggas wanna test my G?" I fumed.

I reached deeper inside the stash spot and grabbed the two twelve inch shanks that I kept on deck for violations like this. Those fuck niggas were about to get it for every slimy muthafucka who had ever crossed me.

The anger inside of me manifested in hot beads of sweat across my forehead. I was strapped and ready to body two niggas who were supposed to be my mans. I didn't know which of them had stolen from me so I planned to ride on the both of them to assure that I punished the right one.

I ripped my bed sheet into strips and used one long piece on each hand to tie a shank to it. I wanted to be certain it would not slip from my grasp once I began sticking holes in muthafuckas chests.

Just as I was finishing up, I heard a soft rap on my cell door. My head snapped around and my senses heightened. Maybe they were coming to serve me before I could serve them.

Let's make it do what it do!

I was in straight killa mode until I saw who was standing outside my door.

"Unc, come on in," I called out.

Jabbo, one of the most respected men at the prison, stood in the doorway. He had been on lock for twenty calendars. He was doing his bid like a real nigga. He didn't fuck with any homo shit, didn't snitch, and tolerated no disrespect. I'd heard that the way he got down in prison was the same way he rocked on the streets back in the late 80's when his crew, the infamous Carver Homes Posse, had ATL in a headlock.

"How was your visit, nephew?" he asked.

"Aight," I muttered in monotone.

Jabbo instantly picked up on the vibe.

"What's the business?" he probed coming up a little closer with a raised brow.

"Bitch ass niggas trying me. Like, they think shit is sweet." I gave him the rundown.

"Think before you make your move because at least one of them is innocent. Never allow your emotions to lead you. That's what got me cased up," he advised.

"I feel you, woady, but right now I'm not tryna hear it," I walked right pass him, headed to Stack's cell at the end of the second tier.

I moved with a singular purpose. When I reached my destination, I found Stack in his cell with his back to the door, reading a magazine.

"I want my shit, woady." My tone was murderous.

"Say what?" he replied, turning to face me.

"You heard me!" I was in no mood to repeat myself. I raised my right hand and brought it down in an arc. "I'm not the one to steal from!" I plunged the sharpened metal into his chest, again and again.

Sweat poured from my forehead as blood spilled from his body. "What the fuck, man?" He stumbled in an attempt to get away.

I quickly swept his legs out from under him with a vicious leg sweep, and he crashed to the floor. Niggas backed out of the way as I pounced on him and gritted, "Punk muthafucka! I'll kill about mine!" I shoved the shank deep into his gut.

As the blood painted his T-shirt red, Solange was the furthest thought from my mind.

Ca$h

Chapter 6
Solange

I was stressed out thinking about the shit that went down with me and Prince. My mind was going every which-a-way but straight, and I was cramping hella bad.

I was struggling to come up with the right plan to win Prince's heart back. I could tell from the poison I'd heard in his voice that the love and devotion he once felt for me had turned into hate. He probably felt that I was heartless, but that wasn't exactly true.

Before I met Prince, I had been dogged out by a long succession of niggas whom I had given my heart to. I had been searching for love while they were only interested in selling dreams and blowing my back out. So, I began playing niggas for their money, and I promised myself that I would never love again. Then I met Prince.

The way he spoiled me and showed his devotion put my heart at conflict with my mind. I began to love him, but I was afraid to give him my all because I didn't want to be hurt again. I kept thinking that as soon as I surrendered my heart to him completely, he would hurt me like men before him had.

My granny had told me to always expect the worst out of men. Hell, Granddaddy treated her like shit, so she would know. In fact, every female I knew had a sad story to tell about what some trifling man had done to them.

By the time I hooked up with Prince, I could've matched those women story for story. Niggas had done me so wrong. I even tried females for a while. That shit didn't turn out to be my cup of tea. I switched back to men, but I was definitely jaded.

Lying on my bed with Asia asleep beside me, I went through the photos that I had saved in my phone as I concentrated on those of me and Prince in happier times.

A knock at the front door was followed by Mr. Sam's voice. "You home?" he called out.

I hopped up out of bed agitated. *Damn, what does he want?*

I opened the front door and flashed a phony smile.

"Hi, Mr. Sam," I greeted.

"I'm sorry to bother you, but this morning I was on my porch reading the AJC when a Chinese looking woman drove up in a little blue car and asked if you lived here. She looked like she had Chinese and black blood in her. She was mixed with something," he said scratching the top of his head.

"Oh, I'm not sure who that could have been. Well, if she needs me she can come back."

"Okay. I was just letting you know in case it was something you needed to know about."

"Thanks."

"Alright. Now if you ever get lonely, I'll be more than happy to come keep you company." His eyes were focused on my cleavage.

"O-kay," I stuttered and slowly closed the door, thinking, *You old freaky bastard. Probably can't even get stiff without a whole bottle of Viagra.*

I wasn't away from the door a good three minutes when there was another knock. *This betta not be Mr. Sam returning to put his mack game down,* I said in my mind.

I returned to the front entrance and politely asked, "Who is it?"

No one replied.

I looked through the peephole and saw an unfamiliar Asian looking chick on the other side of my door. I opened the door and looked her up and down. She wore a lavender wrap-around dress and silver and lavender stilettos.

Sweeping back a long jet-black bang, she asked, "Are you Solange?"

I frowned with a slight attitude because I didn't know her from a can of paint and she was disturbing the hell out of me. "Who needs to know?" I was getting a bad vibe from this bougie chick.

34

"I'm Johanna, Jamal's wife. He's been calling your house phone from the cell phone that I purchased for him. I got your address from the operator since you weren't listed as private. Jamal keeps denying that he knows you. Since I can't get the truth out of him, I decided to come and confront you."

"Oh, did you now?" I balled up my fist ready to introduce her to these hands of mine.

When did bitches get so bold? I guess she didn't know whose house she was coming to! But she was quickly about to find out.

"Excuse me, Boo Thang," I said, stepping out onto the porch. "I know you're not coming to my crib questioning me about your punk ass little husband."

"Uh, duh." She got jazzy out the mouth as if she didn't see me taking off my hoop earrings.

Once I had removed them I said, "Honey, do you want to step inside and get this ass whooping or would you prefer it where you're standing?"

"I didn't come here to fight." She backed down, but by then I was all over that ass.

"You had no business coming here at all!" I drew back and swung at her face with everything I had.

Whap!

The first blow caught her in the nose.

"Oww!" she cried.

"Ol' two cent ass bitch." Whap! "Don't come to my muthafuckin' door no more!" Whap! Whap!

While my fists were pounding her in the head, I grabbed a handful of her hair, twisted it around my hand to hold her head still, and then I beat her down mercilessly.

I recalled Jamal telling me that he didn't have a woman. For six months he had been lying. Whap! I uppercutted his bitch for the lie he had told. Boo Thang grabbed a hold of my weave and tried to pull me down. The next thing I knew we had fought our way from my porch to the front yard. Ol' girl tripped over a huge rock in my flowerbed, and I started putting in work on that ass. She was on the ground waddling like a pig in shit.

"Get off of me!" she wailed.

Her dress had crept up to her titties and all of her shaved pussy was showing. The bitch called herself coming to check me and hadn't put a lick of drawers on.

"Woo, Lawd! That's a pretty ass," Mr. Sam shouted from his front porch across the street .

I looked up at him with my mouth twisted and my forehead creased. "If you want some white trash I'll dump it in your front yard." I dragged her across the lawn by the hair. "Ho, next time you better Google a bitch!" I spewed before giving her one last kick in the face.

Coming over here to confront me about that nigga!

Tired of kicking her pitiful ass, I dusted myself off and went back in the house. I didn't even stop to look back to see if Mr. Sam would go help that stupid ho' up.

Chapter 7
Solange

"**O**h, hell nawl!" I exclaimed, noticing that I had broken a nail. So I stormed back outside and stomped another mud hole in Boo Thang's ass.

When I was done with her she looked a hot mess. Mr. Sam had to pull me off of her and help the skank back to her car.

Back inside my house, I popped an Advil for the headache I caught after all of that commotion. I plopped down on the couch to calm my heaving chest. Again, I began thinking about Prince. When he was home, nothing like this ever happened. He was a good protector and provider.

Before the Advil could muc kick in, Asia awoke and came into the living room whining for breakfast as usual that Saturday morning. "Stop acting like a big baby and go in the kitchen and fix your own breakfast. You know how to cook in the microwave and you can put some bread in the toaster," I said.

She stood there in her Dora the Explorer nightgown crying, "I want you to do it, Mommy."

"If I do, Reverend Ike was a prophet," I quipped with my legs curled flipping through the television stations searching for a good movie. The sarcasm may have gone over her head, but my tone related its meaning.

Asia turned up her nose and spun to head to the kitchen.

"Who are you turning your nose up at?" I asked as I stood up. I went over and slapped her little Prince looking ass across the back.

She wailed like I had damaged her spine, but her little funky butt was putting on an act. "Go brush your teeth and wash your face. Then you can fix you something to eat," I said.

While Asia was preoccupied, I found a pen and some stationary and flopped back down on the couch before I began a letter to Prince.

Baby Daddy,

I miss you and I need you so very much. With you in my life the seas of life were calm and majestic. Without you, every day is a tidal wave of bullshit, drama, and uncertainty. I know that I have let you down, but please blame that on circumstances, not my heart. When you were here, I had grown to depend on you so much that when you went away I didn't know how to make it on my own. I know that you don't want to hear none of that, but it's true. You gave me so much; not just material things but also your love and protection. Now that it's time for me to return it, I have failed miserably. I'll be honest, sometimes I find myself wanting to die.

Tears stained the letter as I poured out my heart. I really didn't want to live any longer.

My cell phone rang from inside the bedroom, interrupting the self-pity party going on inside my head. I dashed down the hallway to answer before the caller hung up.

Short of breath I answered, "Hello?"

"What it do, lil' mama? This is Shaheed."

I searched my memory for a face to put with the name. *Shaheed? Shaheed? Shaheed? Oh, the dude that drives that Dodge Challenger,* I instantly recalled brightening up. Ol' boy was an official baller as well as a prime trick. Just what a bitch needed in her life.

"Hi. I'm doing okay, I guess."

"You sound kind of down, shawdy. Let me come through and scoop you up and see if I can change your mood with a serious shopping spree," he offered.

"You would do that for me?" I downplayed the affect that I knew I had on him from the moment we were introduced by Tash, who kicks it with Shaheed's boy Renegade.

"Of course," he replied without hesitation.

The second I got off the phone with Shaheed, I called Mama and bribed her into coming to get Asia.

"I want a new wig and a purse," she said.

"Mama, I got you. Will you please hurry up? My date will be here in an hour and a half, and I don't want Asia all in the way," I complained.

"Hush, chile. I'm on the way."

"Thank you, Mommie," I sang out and hung up.

All thoughts of Prince were momentarily pushed aside as I sensed the golden opportunity to sink my claws into a prime time cake daddy.

I hurriedly packed Asia up and shipped her off with Mama. Then I gathered up the letter that I had begun to Prince and hid it in my dresser drawer in case Shaheed was one of those nosey type niggas. I was not about to blow my come up.

A ten minute shower left me feeling revived from the altercation with Boo Thang a while ago. I lathered my body with Cherry Blossom by Bath & Body Works. I sprayed the same scent of mist all over me and inhaled it's fragrance. I smelled so good that Shaheed's dick was sure to salute a bitch as soon as he took a whiff.

I pulled on a light blue halter along with a pair of DKNY coochie cutting shorts that advertised my plump pussy print, and slid my small pretty feet into a pair of four inch heeled sandals that showed off my French pedi and my platinum and diamond ankle bracelet.

An hour later, Shaheed pulled up in a brand new Dodge Challenger bumpin' a Lil' Wayne mixtape. He came to the door and said, "Happy Saturday, baby doll." His voice held a deep baritone as he presented me with an assortment of roses inside a pretty glass vase. He licked his sexy and sensual Ludacris lips.

I saw his eyes caress my body, focusing on the 'V' between my thighs. *Trick on deck!* Ran through my mind.

"Thank you, Baby." I smiled and sat the vase on my living room's end table and proceeded out of the door. "So, where are we going?"

"I'ma take you out to Lennox Mall and let you buy that bitch out," he boasted, not realizing what type of hurt I planned to put on his pockets.

"Ooh wee!" I squealed with excitement and poked my booty out as I walked to his whip.

On the way to Lennox, Shaheed hammered me with questions about Prince. Agitated, I replied, "If you don't mind, can we talk about something else?"

The irritation in my voice should have been obvious, but apparently he didn't catch on. He pressed on with another question about Prince.

"How much time did they give him? I heard he caught a life sentence, but some niggas say he caught twenty years."

"Life," I dryly responded.

"That's fucked up. Then again, that was stupid as fuck what he did. Fuck he body a nigga for in front of witnesses? He was making enough dough to pay some goons to handle that. I mean, he wasn't stackin' like *me*, but still."

I rolled my eyes and turned up the volume on the sound system to drown him out. Didn't he know that he didn't have to belittle Prince to get the pussy? All he had to do was close his mouth, and I was going to give him some of this wet wet.

I can't deny that I'm a gold digger, but I couldn't just let him clown my baby's daddy. Ughhh!

I was a split second away from pulling his damn card when he said, "Aight, let me back up off yo' dude 'cause I see you're gettin' tight about it."

"Thank you."

He reached over and rubbed my thigh in a gesture of peace, I guess. The rest of the ride was without conflict. Shaheed told me that he wanted to spoil me rotten. "But you'll have to be devoted. It's one hunnid or nothin'," he declared.

40

"Baby, I do devoted real well," I bragged and gave him a sexy wink.

When we reached the mall, I hit the stores hard, spending Shaheed's d-boy money on five pairs of skinny leg Joes jeans, three pairs of Gucci pumps, a Gucci handbag, and an expensive pair of oversized Chloe sunglasses. I was even able to slide in the purse for Mama without arousing Shaheed's suspicion.

Since he was no longer hating on Prince, and had laced a chick real good, I planned to take him back to my place and show my appreciation. And if I was lucky, I could get a nut myself.

Shaheed altered my plans a bit when he suggested that we chill in a suite at the Hilton in Buckhead.

"Sounds good to me." I didn't hasten to agree.

We entered the Presidential suite holding hands like familiar lovers. I was overwhelmed to find rose petals leading from the door to the bedroom of the suite.

"I called one of my boys while you were shopping and had him to hook it up," he explained.

"You're sooo romantic," I cooed, putting my finger in my mouth and batting my eyes naughtily.

We settled in and ordered a seafood platter. After we were done eating, I went into the bathroom to freshen up while he sat on the bed and sparked a blunt. When I returned from the bathroom, a towel was all that covered my most precious assets.

I stopped right in front of Shaheed and let the towel fall to the floor. He got all bug eyed when he saw my bald kitty kat. He pulled me to him and placed his nose on my mound and breathed in my freshness. "Yes, sirrrrr!" He sang his approval.

Then he stood up and stripped down to his boxers.

"Don't stop now," I egged him on.

He dropped his boxers revealing a—a—a damn wee wee half the size of my pinky finger. It definitely was a wee wee because a dick is not that small. "Are you serious?" I giggled before I realized it.

I covered my mouth like, *oops!*

"I'm sorry. That was ugly," I quickly apologized.

I expected a slap across the face for clowning his little dude, but Shaheed ignored my statement and gave me a smirk.

"It ain't the size of the ship, baby doll," he confidently countered.

Ship? Nigga, you ain't even got a row boat, I thought to myself. *Well, I'm here, coochie all ready. I might as well roll with it,* I decided.

Shaheed eased me down on the bed and kissed his way down my body, starting at my neck. He used a skilled finger to lightly trace circles around my clit while tenderly devouring my nipples. By the time he attended to my bald paradise, my pleasure spot was throbbing with anticipation. I had forgotten all about his *little* problem.

The nigga ate my pussy so damn good, I wanted to ask him for his mother's phone number, so I could call her up and thank her for giving birth to his ass. When he pushed my legs all the way over my head and snaked his tongue inside my booty hole, I cried out his name while gasping for breath.

Moments later, I felt something small and stiff ease into my back passage. The dick was short but the nigga's wind was longer than The Nile River. "Oh my God! Fuck this ass daddy. Make me bust off," I exploded as he jabbed in and out.

Just as a big orgasm was about to come down, I moaned, "Oh yes, Prince. Fuck me good, baby."

"Prince?" snarled Shaheed.

Chapter 8
Prince

I wiped the sweat off my bare chest and flexed my well-defined six pack after finishing my daily workout in the hole. A long bead of perspiration that escaped the towel trickled across the *Trained To Go* tat that is inked across my stomach in English lettering.

I'm tatted up, sleeved up, the whole nine. *Loyalty over Er'thing* reads the tat across my chest. Those two sheisty niggas, Stack and Dushay, should have took those words to heart and then maybe they wouldn't be laid up in the infirmary.

I stabbed Stack first because he was more of a threat to fight back than Dushay's soft ass. True story, when Dushay saw the killer's look in my eyes as I approached him grasping a bloody shank, he yelled out like a bitch and bolted down the tier.

I caught up with that ass and left him wiggling on the floor. "Anybody else wanna test my gangsta?" I challenged the entire cell block.

Jabbo slid up to me and whispered, "Prince, you gotta get out of those bloody clothes and get rid of those tools before the goon squad arrives."

As I slowly walked back to my cell to clean myself up, I heard him bark, "Ain't nobody seen a goddamn thing! You talk you die. On my mother!"

Somebody must've talked because the warden and the goon squad came and put me in the hole the next day. But I knew Jabbo would deal with whoever snitched me out. I also trusted that he would hold down the weed that I left with him.

Anyway, I took a bird bath in the sink then sat down on my bunk and stared at the letter I'd just received from Solange. I didn't even bother reading it; I realized that the bitch wasn't nothin' but a ho that I tried to wife. A nigga just wanted to give Asia something most children in the hood don't have, a two parent home. Ya heard me.

I was considering opening Solange's letter just to see what new lies she had to tell when I heard someone slide back the metal flap that covered the small rectangular window in the door.

A pretty set of brown eyes looked in on me.

"Prince Myers?" she asked.

I acknowledged my full government name with a slight nod of my head. From the back of the cell where I now stood, her voice was barely audible.

"Please come to the cell door so that I won't have to yell for you to hear me," instructed Lieutenant Wright much more politely than I was used to hearing officers speak. Her tone was somewhere in-between prissy and educated.

I instantly disliked her.

I slowly stepped to the door, taking my time. "Sup?" I muttered when I got there.

She stared at me through the small window for a minute, cleared her throat in a feminine sort of way, and replied, "My name is Lieutenant Wright, and I'm the duty officer this evening." Which meant that she was the highest rank on duty at the time. "Are you doing okay?"

"I'm good."

"Is there anything that I can help you with this evening?"

"Nah." I grilled her for being too fucking pretty. Just like dirty-ass Solange. "You can't help me with nothin'," I snorted.

"Well, maybe if you tell me what happened I'll be able to help you," she said.

I wasn't receptive to that though. I took it as if the bitch was asking me to snitch on myself. So I mean-mugged her even harder. She continued to offer her assistance until I concluded that she was jocking my swag. In another place, at another time, I might've leaped at the opportunity to put my mack down on her, but the uniform reminded me that she was the popo.

"I already told you that I'm good," I repeated more sternly.

My eyes gazed into hers, and what I saw in her stare was something much more than official inquiry. Finally, she told me that she would be back to check on me again in a week, but I had the feeling that she would find a reason to return much sooner. Her eyes spoke a million words that her mouth didn't utter.

"Don't waste ya time," I said, and turned my back. If she was still staring, I'm sure she saw the Tommy Gun tatted across my back with *Fuck the police* tatted underneath.

Though Lieutenant Wright was not an actual police, I considered anyone who wore a badge to be popo.

I heard her frustration come out through a sigh as she closed the metal flap over the cell door's window. But I didn't give a damn. If she expected me to hop on her bra strap like the other niggas who were on lock with me, she had the game all fucked up.

Ca$h

Chapter 9
Nicole

My heart threatened to leap clear out of my chest as I walked back to my office trying to control my excited breathing. Oh my God! It was really him! I had thought so two weeks ago when I saw him while making my rounds through the cell blocks. I had glanced up on the second tier in E-block, and saw him leaning haphazardly on the rail frowning down at me.

Even with the scowl on his face, he was as thuggishly handsome as he was five years ago when I first encountered him. From that day forward, his face had remained in my mind as if it was painted under my eyelids. Two weeks ago, I had only caught a quick glimpse of him in E-block, and it had been from a distance. I wasn't absolutely certain that it was him. However, when I looked inside his cell in the hole and saw him standing there bare chested, perspiration dripping from his muscled physique, I knew for sure it was him.

The memory of the first time I laid eyes on him came flashing back. I was up in Atlanta visiting a friend who had just had a baby. Leaving her house that was located in a crime-ridden part of the city known as the Bluff, my car suddenly broke down two blocks from my friend's house.

It was dark out so I was a little apprehensive when a stranger offered his assistance. Since I knew nothing about fixing a car, and was desperate to get away from the Bluff, I naively accepted his offer. Minutes later, the stranger had a knife to my throat and was forcing me inside his vehicle. "If you scream I'll cut your muthafuckin' throat," he warned.

As if heaven sent, I heard a voice say, "Leave her alone or *she* won't be the victim tonight."

"Mind your business, nigga," my assailant growled.

"I'm making it my business," my guardian angel replied pointing a gun at the man's head. "Let her go, bruh. This is your last warning."

The knife was removed from against my throat.

"Now mash out, nigga, before I open up your chest plate," snarled my rescuer. The stranger with the knife took off running.

"You okay, shawdy?" my savior asked, comforting me with a friendly hug.

"I was so afraid." I stood there and wept, still shaking with tears even though my assailant had been chased away. "I want to call the police and report this incident," I told him, but he made his opinion of the matter quickly known.

"Miss Lady, I don't fuck with the popo. I'll call up a mechanic I know to get your car straight. I'll sit right here with you until you're on your way safely, but if you gotta involve the police, I'm out. Trust, the dude that just attacked you will get what he has coming, they always do," he assured.

He also kept his promise to remain with me until I was safely on my way home. "Now stay your pretty self out of neighborhoods like this," he lightly chastised, then placed a soft kiss on my cheek before waving goodbye.

I was on the interstate headed back to Statesboro when I realized that he had never told me his name.

"*Prince Myers*," I said aloud, now that I knew his name. It tasted like the sweet nectar of a Georgia peach on the tip of my tongue. The name *Prince* fit him perfectly.

I turned on my computer and typed his name into a file that was already set to show each inmate at the prison. My heart sunk when I saw that he had been convicted of murder and was sentenced to life.

Next, I pulled up his visitation list and saw that he had a girlfriend and a daughter approved to visit him. I wondered if his girl was holding him down under the present circumstances.

Chapter 10
Solange

Check out time was at eleven o'clock in the morning. Shaheed and I showered together then we both got dressed, beating the clock by twenty minutes.

Last night I had sucked his little man real good to make up for calling him my baby's daddy's name. Then I rode him reverse cowgirl style and my slip of tongue was erased from his thoughts. Or so I thought.

"Aye, lil' mama, I know you and Prince been together for a minute, but you're gonna have to get over that nigga if you wanna be mine. I want a rider who is down for me and only me. If you can't commit to that let me know now," said Shaheed as he drove me home.

I considered everything before answering him. I mean, he had a mean tongue game, and he was long winded with that Jolly Rancher sized dick of his. His thickness couldn't fill a bitch up, and being with him would surely leave me wanting more size. I looked around and caught a glimpse of the half dozen shopping bags on the backseat. The midget dick nigga had bankrolls to make up for his shortcomings.

I perked up, figuring I could always buy myself some toys with the length and equipment to help Shaheed out.

I put on my best smile and replied, "You know I'm a rider. I stayed grinding with my baby's daddy, and when he needed me I was always there."

He snorted. "Why you keep bringing Prince up? Fuck that nigga. He's bagged up for a long time. I'm only interested in me and you."

"Awww. I'm sorry, sweetie, you're getting jealous," I stated and cut my eyes over at him to see his expression. He was definitely in his feelings with the long wrinkle that creased his forehead.

"Nawl. I'm not jealous of no nigga on God's green earth."

I reached over and rubbed his arm with the palm of my hand to calm him down even though he tried to front like he wasn't jealous. "Good. Baby, you don't need to be 'cause you're a boss. I promise I'm going to fall in line." I was only trying to boost his ego.

"A'ight, I'ma hold you to it."

"Please do," I said as I picked his hand up and placed it between my thighs and dead on top of my coodie.

A few minutes passed when Shaheed answered a call on his cell phone. I reached over in my handbag and checked my text messages while he was talking.

Sup, ma? U missing me? read the first text that I opened. It was from bitch ass Jamal.

I frowned and let out a long sigh and replied, *Hell no asshole! You better find that bitch you married!*

He texted back, *Stop trippin' I wanna come over and beat that pussy up.*

I quickly glanced over at Shaheed to make sure he wasn't paying me any attention. He was still involved in his own conversation so I sent Jamal another text. *Nigga, fuck you!* Then I turned my phone off.

I put my phone inside of my handbag and ear hustled on Shaheed's conversation to see if he was already talking to the next bitch. He had stressed hard to me that I would have to be completely devoted to him in order to be his girl, but that didn't mean he would be devoted to me. Every nigga I'd kicked it with before Prince, was a straight up ho.

To my pleasure it didn't sound as if he was talking to a chick. Listening to his end of the conversation I concluded that he was discussing street business.

At my house, he helped me carry the shopping bags inside. "I'ma fall back through later, a'ight?" he said, kissing me goodbye.

"That's cool with me," I replied as I opened the car door to exit.

As soon as Shaheed left, I called Tash.

"Gurrlll, let me tell you about your man's dude, Shaheed," I babbled sitting on the side of my bed with my legs crossed. "He came through and took me shopping yesterday and let me buy the mall out. Then we went to the hotel and, gurrlll…"

By the time I finished recounting my night Tash was laughing so hard I could picture the tears running down her face.

"Dayum! Shaheed is all buff with muscles and packing an inch worm!" she commented.

We both cracked up. Then I pointed out, "Renegade is buff too."

"But he's not cursed with a bite size. Trust, my boo's dick is that super-size deluxe."

I grew quiet for a few seconds, scandalously imagining a big ten inch muscle between Renegade's legs, and him stretching me wide open with it.

"Trick, don't even think about it. I would fuck you up," said Tash, reading me like only a bestie can.

Later, I was sprawled out on the couch in hot yellow boy shorts and a white baby tee when Mama called for me to pick Asia up.

"No, Mommy. Will you please keep her one more day? I'll pay you fifty dollars." I tried to bribe her.

"Did you get my wig and purse?" she asked with her deep sultry southern voice.

I chuckled. "Yes, Mommy, I did. My God, you're so thirsty that it's not even funny.

"You're getting yours. I gotta get mine."

I laughed. "I'm not even mad at you. Who do you think I get my ways from?" I hinted.

"Ooookay!" she sang.

It was late evening when Shaheed returned. As soon as I let him in he saw my pussy print on display. He licked his lips and quipped. "What's for dinner?"

"Some coochie served any way you like it," I purred, guiding him to the bedroom by the hand.

A short while later, Shaheed held my thighs wide apart and used his tongue to make a trail up my leg to the center of my mounting passion. *Sweet Jesus!* I was going to end up sprung on an iddy biddy dick trick. I was not going to go there.

Stick to your script, bitch, and don't let your pussy guide you or you'll end up with nothing but a broken heart and a wet ass, I reminded myself.

When Shaheed's skilled tongue traced delicate figure S's around my pulsating clit, I wondered if I could keep my sanity, let alone continue to run game on him. He ate my coochie so good I cried out, "Baby, it feels so—so supa crazy goddamn fucking good I wanna scream!" After three mega intense orgasms I was pulling my hair out. Shaheed smacked his lips savoring my sweetness. He stood up and removed a gun from his waist, placing it on the nightstand by the bed.

That was the type of thuggish shit that turned a bitch on even more. I helped him out of his True Religion jeans and his black boxers. His little soldier looked like the thumb of a hitchhiker.

"You gonna return the favor?" he needlessly asked. Because of the way he had just ate me out, I owed his entire bloodline some head.

I stepped right to my business, showing him that I'm a boss bitch. Before long, I had his legs over his head tonguing his asshole. The nigga was squirming and moaning like we had switched genitals and now *he* was the bitch.

I heard a noise at my back. When I looked over my shoulder, Jamal was standing there pointing a gun at us.

I let out an ear-piercing scream. Shaheed shot straight up and reached for his heater, but it was no longer on the nightstand.

Jamal gave us a grin that was full of evil and snickered. "Yo, son, you lookin' for this, yo?" He pointed Shaheed's own gun at us. "Get up and kiss the carpet, nigga," he growled.

While Shaheed followed his command I appealed, "Jamal, why you doing all this? And how did you get into my house?"

"Shut up slut bucket ass ho! I had an extra door key made dumb bitch," he responded then slapped me to the floor.

He put the gun to my head and added, "You know what the move is."

I shivered as I sent a silent prayer up to heaven, hoping God wouldn't abandon me though I only called on him in times of need.

"Thank you, Lord." I sighed with relief when the gun was removed from against my head.

I laid still while Jamal robbed Shaheed for his money and jewelry. "This is what you get when you fuck a rat bitch. The ho set you up, kid," lied Jamal, then he cracked Shaheed's head open with the butt of the gun.

"I'm not hard to find," he gritted, backing out of the bedroom.

I sat on the edge of the bed crying into my hands, trying to convince Shaheed and Renegade that I had nothing to do with the robbery.

Shaheed had called his man over as soon as Jamal left. My girl Tash had came along, *luckily for me*, I thought. I could tell that Shaheed believed me from the way he comforted me while I cried on his shoulder, but Renegade mean mugged me and looked at me like he was still skeptical.

"Why would I do something like that?" I kept asking in my own defense.

Renegade said to Shaheed, "Straight up, fam, I don't trust this broad. Number one, she's too thirsty. Number two, shawdy, ain't got no love for a nigga. That nigga, Prince, gave her the world on a silver platter. As soon as he caught a bid, she fucked up his stash and started fucking out of both pants legs. So, what does she care about you?"

I looked at Shaheed, and the expression on his face told me that his faith in my honesty was weakened by Renegade's words. I turned to Tash for support.

"Tash, you've known me since middle school. Tell them I don't get down like that."

"I don't get involved in my man's affairs." She stood in my bedroom's doorway scrolling through her cell phone like I wasn't pleading for my life.

If my eyes were bullets, I would've blown that trick's cheap tracks back.

"Fam, you can't see this jump off for what she really is because the "P" got you fucked up in the head. So just fall back and let me deal with her snake ass," Renegade said, trying hard to convince Shaheed.

Renegade pulled out a chrome gun and shoved it under my chin. "Rat ass ho, you think this is a game," he said with a heavy growl.

I squeezed my eyes shut and waited to hear the pow.

Chapter 11
Nicole

I awoke from my dream with moistness in my panties and aching in my nipples for his lips to devour them. I shouldn't have been lying next to my husband of three years dreaming about another man. An convict at that!

I couldn't get Prince out of my mind. I closed my eyes and imagined him holding me in his arms. "Umm," I moaned.

"Huh? What did you say?" asked Anthony, placing the article down that he was reading. My husband was a medical surgeon. He was forty-seven years old, twenty years my senior. If Prince was a ten, Anthony was about a six. He was a large man with average looks and a very serious demeanor. I had never been in love with him, but I did love him and he adored me.

To be quite honest, I married Anthony because I knew that I would not have to worry about him cheating on me, and we would not have financial struggles. Had I chosen to, I could have been a housewife, but I wasn't the type of woman who's allergic to work.

"No, honey, I didn't say anything," I half truthfully, replied.

"Well, I'm going to sleep, I'm exhausted. Do you need this?" he considerately asked me.

"No, hun."

He switched off the lamp beside the bed. Five minutes later, he was snoring like a bear. For some reason, I was annoyed by his snoring, although usually I was only slightly irritated by it. Deep down I knew it was because I was thinking of that bad boy at the prison, comparing Anthony to Prince.

Prince intrigued me and had me wanting to know more about him. Anthony had become boring, and I finally admitted it to myself as I got out of bed, went into the study, and switched on my PC.

I went to the appropriate site, pulled up Prince's profile, and stared at his face for at least five minutes.

A tap on my shoulder startled me. "Come back to bed," Anthony said in a tone that meant he wanted intimacy.

I switched the PC off and went to do my wifely duties. Visions of Prince dancing in my head caused me to long for him in a way that was indecent. Under the circumstances, it was difficult for me to get wet for Anthony. He didn't seem to notice. He pushed right on inside and grunted after eight or nine strokes. I faked an orgasm, shamefully.

A minute later the bear was fast asleep, but my desire for a forbidden fruit was awakened and ready to be fed.

The following evening I could hardly wait for my shift to begin. As soon as I finished briefing the officers under my authority, I made my rounds in the hole to check on the inmates in solitary confinement. Of course, I went to Prince's cell last, hoping that this encounter would turn out better than the last one.

Chapter 12
Prince

I had been in the hole for seventeen days, but the shit didn't bother me. The way I saw it, it was just another part of the prison. In fact, the solitude allowed me time to think and plot my moves.

I got a kite from Jabbo. Woady let me know that he had served justice on the nigga who snitched me out about the stabbings. As for the two niggas I'd stuck holes in, Stack was gonna be gucci. He was a true convict who would rather die than snitch. Word was that Dushay was wearing a shit bag and had been transferred to the medical prison in Augusta, Georgia.

I'd also been informed that Dushay was the one who'd stolen my shit. Stack hadn't been involved in it. So I had to square things with him when I got back on the compound. All I could do was step to him like a man and apologize. If he still wanted blood, I was ready for war.

Jabbo had my weed put up for me, so I was good on that issue. I was thinking about it when I heard the metal flap on the door sliding back.

"Good evening, Inmate Myers. Is there anything I can help you with?"

I stalked to the door and stared at her through the small window. "Lieutenant, I told you last week that I don't need nothin' but to be left the fuck alone. So why you back at my door sweatin' me? Can't you find something else to do? Or are you here on some personal type shit?"

Her face turned blush red, and she quickly shut the flap and stormed off like a rejected lover. *Yep, baby girl is definitely sweating my swag,* but I no longer did pretty bitches.

Ca$h

Chapter 13
Solange

Just when I thought I was a goner, I saw two eyeballs staring through the curtains over my bedroom window. Thank God for nosey ass Mr. Sam! His timing was literally life-saving.

I gazed back at him, and my eyes were pleading for help. He was my only hope for survival because Tash had switched teams on my ass. Renegade stood over me with no sympathy in his eyes, ready to blow me away.

"Whatchu looking at?" Renegade's eyes followed mine.

"Who the fuck is that?" barked Shaheed, catching a glimpse of Mr. Sam before the old man fled.

Tash said, "Renegade, let's leave this trick bitch to be dealt with another day. Whoever peeped in the window will probably call the police, and her ass is not worth the trouble."

"What about my man's money and shit? This ho has to pay for that," he continued to stress.

"She has some money Prince left her. Look under the bed," she told him, and grilled me with her hateful ass. "See, bitch, I wouldn't have shitted on you if you hadn't accused me of telling Prince your business. How you gon' come at me wit' some dumb shit like that?" she asked me and twisted her neck toward Renegade. "Get that money, baby, so we can get ghost."

My mouth flew open! No, she didn't just encourage him to take my paper, I thought to myself, panicking. Why had I told that bitch about the ninety-seven thousand dollars I had stashed? Not even Prince knew that I still had money of his; I had lied to him about getting robbed. Shit, he was in prison. Asia and I needed more money than he did.

Shaheed got down on his knees and looked under the bed. He drug out the three shoe boxes that contained the money. My heart sank to the floor.

"Bingo," he exclaimed, smiling triumphantly when he lifted up the tops and looked inside.

Bam! Renegade hit me in the back of the head so hard with the gun I was sure that my skull was fractured. I was dazed but even more disoriented from the loss of my money. How could me and Asia survive now?

Tash strutted over to me and spat, "Bitch, you ain't shit. You're just a money thirsty pigeon ass ho. Shaheed was really feeling your phony ass." She mushed my face back with the palm of her hand.

The only reason I didn't spring up and be on that ass like white on rice was because Renegade kept the gun aimed at me. My eyes burned with fury as I silently vowed to tear Tash's ass to shreds when I caught her alone. I wouldn't have ever imagined that she would flip on me.

It's all good. Payback is a mutha!

Chapter 14
Nicole

"**H**e is such an arrogant butthole!" I complained to Raven, my dearest friend in the entire world.

She poo-pooed me like she'd always done when I was having a white girl moment. Afterwards, she might laugh and tease me for being so theatrical, but she never turned a deaf ear to me when I wanted to vent.

"Calm down, Nicole, and tell me what Anthony did," she empathized.

"Anthony didn't do anything, I was referring to Prince. Gosh! I can't stand him."

"Yeah, right," she mocked, rolling her eyes up at the ceiling, teasingly.

I had already told her all about him and how we met. Now I told her how rude he was to me earlier.

"Dang, that's turning me on. Like yourself, I love the bad boy type," she teased.

I held up two fingers like a pitchfork. "Don't play! I'll poke your eyes out," I warned as we sat across from each other on stools in her kitchen. "Besides, I may need him to put it on me 'cause Anthony's belly is getting bigger by the day. Soon I'll have to hold it up with my knees while we are screwing. Gurl, it's about to be a mess."

Raven giggled so hard that tears streamed from her eyes. "I promise not to go to the prison and steal your *prince*," she clowned. "Cause it sounds like you may need him as a backup plan in the near future."

I play-punched her in the shoulder. I then leaned on her kitchen counter and plucked a white grape out of a bowl of fruit that was within arm's reach.

"Did you remind him where you all met?" she asked.

"No. I didn't get a chance to because he was so mean to me." I made a puppy dog face and continued smacking on the grape.

"Maybe that's a good thing, Nicole. After all, you are a married woman. Hellooooo! For real, maybe you should just leave it alone. This has potential to 'cause big trouble."

I nodded in agreement. "I think you're right," I conceded and changed subjects.

While Raven told me about her lesbian co-worker coming on to her, I was only half listening. I was so preoccupied with the question of whether or not Prince found me attractive. I was further wondering, if the Solange chic on his visitation list had his heart.

Just the thought of him being in love with her made me nauseous. *Why am I being so ridiculous? He is not my man.* I promised myself I would keep a safe distance from inmate, Prince Myers. That Solange woman could have his arrogant ass. I had a husband who adored me. I must learn to be content with that, I chastised myself, massaging my temples to rub away the stress that the whole ordeal had brought on.

Chapter 15
Solange

Last night after Shaheed and his crew left, the police arrived at my door saying that they had received a call alerting them of a possible robbery or aggravated assault taking place at my address. "No officers, everything is fine here." I tried to mislead them, but my bruised face and wild hair must have drawn their suspicion.

"Ma'am, we're going to have to come inside and look around," asserted the taller of the white police officers.

I sighed and stepped aside, allowing them to enter.

I had up-righted all of the furniture that Renegade had knocked over when he was throwing me around the house. So, with the exception of the bruises on my neck and face, everything looked to be kosher. Of course, cops are suspicious and trained to sense when a person is lying, and those two were no different.

However, no matter how hard they pressed, I maintained that everything was fine. I was determined to get my payback in my own manner. Real bitches don't snitch.

After finally getting rid of the boys in blue, I flopped across my bed with thoughts of nothing but revenge on my mind. Damn, I thought Tash had my back. We were supposed to be better than the bullshit.

Last night showed me that you can't see a snake until you cut your grass. I understood that Renegade was her man and that he paid all of her bills and kept her purse on swole, but they had only been kicking it for a year. She wasn't even his wifey. She was just one of his sideline chicks.

Every time she caught the whorish nigga sniffing up another bitch's ass, whose shoulder did she cry on? Mine. When he blacked her fuckin' eye and spit in her face because he found pictures of her ex in her phone, who was it that held an ice pack on her eye for hours to help the swelling go down? *Me.* I swear some bitches get dick dumb over a nigga and shit all over their lifelong friends.

Trust, that trick had turned me into her enemy.

My head was pounding from stress and the vicious blow that Renegade's punk ass inflicted to the back of my head. I rubbed the soft spot and told myself that his day was coming. Shaheed's too; his ass had left me hanging. He had allowed his man to convince him that I had set him up. Worse than that, had Mr. Sam never peeked through the window, Shaheed was going to stand there and let Renegade shoot me in the head.

I swear niggas ain't shit. To think I was really feeling that little half of a hotdog having dick nigga. Now him, his man, and Tash were on my shit list.

I got out of bed, went into the bathroom and searched the medicine cabinet for a pain reliever. To my disappointment, there was just a lone pill in the bottle. I needed at least three.

I walked back into the bedroom nearly tripping over my own feet, and plopped back down on the bed. I grabbed my cell phone off the floor, swallowed my pride, and called my older sister, Angie.

"Hello?" she answered on the second ring.

"What's up, sis? This is Solange."

"What? Someone in the family must have died. You never call me unless it's a catastrophe."

She was right, I avoided her bougie ass at all cost.

"No one has died, Angie," I assured her.

"Well, what do you need from me? Because I know this isn't simply a *thinking of you* phone call."

"Look, sis, I'm in a bind. Will you help me out?"

"Uh…I don't know. I hope it's not money that you need."

"No, it's not," I said. "I have a headache so bad I can't move. Will you please bring me some Advil's?"

"Are you pregnant?"

"Girl nawl," I yelled.

"Are you certain," she lightly badgered in her kind of accusatory, judgmental way.

"Hold on," I said, suddenly alarmed.

I darted over to the calendar on the inside of my bedroom door and stared at it with my mouth wide open. My period was a week late!

"Hellooo!" Angie said.

"I'm back," I replied in a worried tone. I was not about to have another rug rat.

"Well, are you?"

"Am I what?"

"Preggo."

"I'm not sure," I admitted. "But I'm a week late."

"Hmmff!" Angie snorted disdainfully. "If you are, do you even know who the father is?"

"You know, I almost told you a thing or two," I replied. I was damn tired of her looking down on me. At thirty-two years old, she was a successful claims attorney for a prestigious insurance company. She was also single, childless, independent, and drove a new modeled '12 750 Beemer. Her condo in Buckhead was laced, and she vacationed in places like Aruba and Spain.

My dear sister didn't have a man, which I figured out long ago was why she was forever hating on me.

"I'm just saying, Solange, you're a hot mess," she attacked.

I took a deep breath and slowly counted to ten.

"Angie while you're getting the Advil, will you grab me an EPT?" I eventually asked, exasperated.

"I guess so, but an ounce of prevention is worth a pound of cure."

I hung up on her.

An hour later, I opened the door to let her in. I didn't even speak before snatching the bag out of her hand and racing off to the bathroom to pee on the EPT stick.

When the results showed a negative reading, I shouted with the joy of a million dollar Lotto winner, and the pounding in my head miraculously vanished. Angie turned her lip up and scoffed, "I don't approve of you letting different men lay with you without using protection. That is just plain nasty."

"Get out of my damn house," I snapped.

She screwed up her face, turned on her heels, and stormed out.

Angie hadn't drove off ten minutes when there was another knock at my door. I looked through the peephole and my hair almost caught on fire.

This nigga has some nerves! I thought, snatching the door open and frowning at Shaheed.

"What the fuck you want?" I hissed, arms folded across my chest.

"I wanna talk to you, baby doll," he had the audacity to reply, while offering me a pink bag from Victoria Secrets.

I knocked the bag of gifts out of his hand and stomped the muthafuckas. Tears poured from my eyes as I roared, "Muthafucka, you got me fucked up! You let the next nigga convince you that I set you up, and then you let him shove a gun in my mouth. A fuckin' gun, Shaheed! Not to mention he almost busted my head, and you robbed me! Nigga, get off my porch," I said before pushing him in the chest.

"Baby, just let me explain."

"Explain?" I asked turning my back to go back inside. "Ain't nothing to explain, you dirty ass bastard!" I exploded going postal on him.

I bared my teeth and slapped the black off his face. I wasn't done yet; I drew my foot back and kicked him in the balls as hard as I could. He yelped and grabbed his nuts. That's when I went in on him, and tried to beat him to death.

My blows couldn't have hurt because he rose up and pinned my arms to my side, lifted me up, and carried me inside.

"Mr. Sam, help! He gon' kill me!" I screamed at the top of my lungs while at the same time swinging my legs back and forth trying to get him to put me down.

"Chill out, shawdy. I'm not gonna hurt you," he softly said, kissing my tears.

"Put me down! I don't trust you. Helppp!"

"Chill, Solange," repeated Shaheed.

As soon as he put me down and released my arms, I clawed his fucking face. "Aww!" he belted out then re-pinned my arms to my side.

"Baby, I apologize for what I let Renegade do to you. My head wasn't right last night. I couldn't think straight, but I should've known my baby wouldn't cross me like that. Shawdy, I don't care what my man thinks of you. I got love for you and I'ma make everything up to you."

I wanted to hawk a glob of spit in his face.

He nibbled on my earlobe and whispered, "I'm sprung on you, baby. C'mon, let me taste your pussy...right now."

I guess he felt that he could handle me like some small minded trick bitch. He didn't know that my game was much tighter than the average ho.

I moaned. "Make love to me, daddy." *So I can rock your ass to sleep later!*

Ca$h

Chapter 16
Prince

I was out of the hole and back in my old cell. They couldn't pin the stabbings on me so I was whistling, *Catch me if you can, like the gingerbread man.*

Like I stated earlier, that snitch nigga, Dushay, was no longer on the compound. He was at a whole 'nother facility that was equipped to attend to his medical needs.

"I bet that fool will think twice from now on before he steals from someone else," predicted Jabbo who was leaned inside the doorway of my cell.

"Bet dat," I agreed.

"Prince, you gotta step to Stack and square things with y'all."

"I'ma do that right away," I replied.

I knocked on Stack's door before entering his cell. He hopped up from his desk, shank in hand.

"Woady, I'm not here on no beef-type shit. I know now that you didn't violate. I reacted too fast, and I apologize for that. Just tell me what I gotta do to make things right between us." I made a few steps toward him with humbleness.

"Just give me a one," he said watching my every movement like he was trying to be sure I wasn't on no fuck shit.

A *one* is an old fashioned one on one fist fight, no weapons, and no homeboys coming to your assistance.

I said, "Stack, I already wronged you. I don't wanna thump with you, big folks, but if you really wanna *hit,* I guess that's how it has to go down."

I took off my shirt.

I can't even front, that old man was nice with them thangs, but my hook game was just a little bit better and my wind was stronger because I had been working out. Plus, I didn't smoke cancer sticks like Stack did.

Jabbo stood at the door running off onlookers whose presence might've caught the attention of the C.O. inside the control booth. Me and Stack bounced each other around the cell then traded punches, blows for blow, until I staggered him with a mean left hook. He grabbed ahold of me to keep from going down. I could've destroyed that ass, but I wasn't tryna shine on him. I was just giving him the head up he asked for.

"That's enough," barked Jabbo.

I let go of Stack and we gave each other a pound.

"You got a nice punch, old man," I acknowledged.

"Yeah, but I gotta give up the cigarettes because my stamina is zero," he confessed, already going to his stash for a smoke.

"When you're ready come down to my cell so we can blaze a blunt," I offered.

The next day I was back on my grind selling zips of weed for street-to-street money transactions. This meant the buyer's people on the street gave the money to my people out there. The only person I had on the outside was Cap, a comrade of mine who had gotten out six months ago. Cap was a solid dude who kept our business square.

I used the pay phone to call Mr. Sam collect. The story he told me about Solange left me heated. That bitch was going to make me send Cap over there to get at her ass if she continued to have all of that drama going on where my daughter rested at.

I was just about to dial Solange's number when the C.O. walked up and told me that I was wanted in the lieutenant's office.

"Which L.T.?" I asked.

"Wright."

"Yeah, whatever!" I scoffed. *Why is this chick calling me to her office? Can't she see I don't wanna chop it up with her?*

A minute later, I stepped into Lt. Wright's office showing nothing but attitude.

"Please close the door," she said, ignoring my hostile posture.

"What you want with me?" I asked after closing the door behind me like she had asked.

She looked at me and said, "You're much different than I imagined you would be."

"Well, stop imagining shit about me."

"You seemed thuggish but nice that night," she reflectively spoke.

I stared at her hard, but there was no recognition beyond seeing her behind the prison's walls. "Man, you don't know me." I disputed her claim.

"You don't recognize me, do you?" She smiled. Then she reminded me how we met a few years back.

"You're bullshittin'," I exclaimed as that night came back to me in clarity. "Dayum, where did you get that new body from? You were sorta thin back then."

"I've been eating my Wheaties," she said. "And I see you've been doing your thug thizzle, unfortunately."

"If you're referring to me being on lock, all I can say is I was put in a situation."

"I'm not judgmental. I know that sometimes things happen. You have to have some good in you or else you wouldn't have come to my aid that night. You were like a prince coming to save me from villains," she reminisced.

"If you say so."

"I'm being honest, but what has turned you so cold?"

"Pretty ass women like you," I told her.

Without much prompting, I gave her a short version of my history with Solange.

"All women aren't evil like that," she defensively remarked.

I sat on the edge of her desk and peered into her eyes. "Tell me something," I began and hesitated for a minute. I wasn't sure if I should ask her my next question, but my curiosity got the best of me. "Are you straight up attracted to me?"

"That's a question I'd rather not answer," she replied in vain because her eyes betrayed her.

"You don't have to answer. What's understood need not be spoken. Just tell me this, if you were in my baby's mama's shoes, would you be true to me?"

"Yes, I would."

I laughed, and then my face contorted into a frown. I grabbed her left hand and pointed to her wedding ring. "Well, why you all on my dick, and you got a husband? Y'all hos ain't shit." I stood up and walked out of her office.

Chapter 17
Solange

I put the pussy on Shaheed like I was screaming for the last time. I sucked his little man below his waist, tongued his nasty crack, and let him come all over my face. Whatever it took to eventually sing him a lullaby.

Evening turned into night, followed by morning. Shaheed dressed, looked me in the eyes, holding my chin up with two fingers, and vowed, "On everything that I love, I'm gone over you, Solange. I'm ready to wife you— just like that." He snapped his fingers and soon after led me outside to his car.

He was driving a plain black Crown Victoria with dark tint on the windows. It was not one of his whips that he flossed in. He popped the trunk and grabbed a large canvas bag. "Here you go, baby doll," he said as he handed over the money that he had taken from me.

A huge burden was lifted off my shoulders. Now I wouldn't have to scrape, beg, and borrow to make it.

"Thank you." I exhaled a long sigh.

"It's all love, shawdy. I even tossed in an extra ten bands to make up for what went down."

"You didn't have to do that."

"Maybe not, but I wanted to keep it one hunnid. Do you promise to do the same?"

"I don't know any other way," I seriously professed.

He grinned at my claim. I could practically see the wheels turning in his mind. He said, "I need you to tell me everything you know about that nigga who ran up on us in your crib."

I didn't hestitate to give him every ounce of information I could provide. "He be hustling over on Ashby and MLK, but he's a barber at the new barber shop near the West End mall," I eagerly disclosed.

"The shop ran by my Muslim brother, Zakee?"

"Yep. He likes to hang out at the strip club called Pin-Ups. You want me to show you the house that he sells weed out of?"

"Yeah, let's ride, shawdy." Shaheed was down.

I was more than happy that Jamal was going to get what he had coming to him. Didn't his slow ass know that he could not get away with what he had done?

Chapter 18
Nicole

Months rolled by. I tried my darnest to get Prince out of my head but doing so was a pointless effort. That man had invaded my thoughts and my dreams. I would see him moving about the prison with a swagger that turned me into a groupie.

The captain had given me the responsibility of investigating reports that Prince was dealing drugs in the institution. Although it compromised my job, I did everything in my power to destroy all evidence—like kites received from informants—that Prince was indeed involved in dealing marijuana. I even put several snitches up for immediate transfer to protect Prince from their deviousness.

Whenever I would pass by him on the compound, my heart would flutter like an infatuated school girl. He would look at me conceitedly and keep it moving as if there could never be anything between us. I wanted to grab him by the shoulders and scream, "Every woman is not trifling!" His last words to me left me feeling like a Jezebel.

I'd been beating myself up for desiring Prince so strongly. Even though I hadn't done anything inappropriate with him, I felt like I had cheated on my husband. It didn't help that Prince had a very low opinion of attractive women, especially of those whom had eyes for someone other than their man.

"He seems to have no concept of a woman realizing that she has married someone who isn't her soul mate," I whined to Raven.

"How can you be sure that Prince is your soul mate? I mean, you don't know much about him at all. What type of future can you have with a man who doesn't even acknowledge you?" she sensibly asked.

I was not deterred. "He acknowledges me, if only to himself. No matter how hard he pretends to be, I can sense that he wants me as much as I want him." I contested to her concerns.

"Okay, but even so, he has life in prison, Nicole. You said it yourself; he must serve a minimum of thirty years."

"I don't care. I can wait."

"Oh, my God! You've lost your mind."

Raven slapped herself across the forehead in total disbelief, but I knew that my girl would have my back no matter what. I told her that I had researched Prince's case. "I believe it has some holes in it. I read over every page of his trial transcript and there were so many contradictions," I mentioned.

I knew what I was talking about because I had studied criminal law in college before deciding that it wasn't for me.

"Nicole, I'm beginning to worry that you might be obsessed," kidded Raven.

"Mark my words, boo boo, I'm going to help my Prince Charming regain his freedom so that I can become Mrs. Myers. Just promise me you'll be my maid of honor."

"For the second time?" she teased.

"And the last one," I sincerely replied.

At home, I sat down in my swivel chair and stared at my computer screen, looking at all the drama going on, on Solange's Facebook page. I went through her photos and saw that she was one of those high maintenance chicks. Her and Prince's daughter was a darling looking little girl, though.

I logged off and pulled Prince's mug shot up on the screen. His frown was a turn on. I concluded that gangstas don't smile for cameras.

Before I knew it, my hand was inside my pj's and my head was tilted back. I was imagining that my finger was Prince's tongue. My back arched as I slowly traced circles around my swelling button of pleasure. I pictured him gripping my hips and feasting on my pie.

"Ahhh yesss!" I began to moan.

My husband's ringtone ruined the moment.

"Yes, dear," I answered, hiding my agitation.

"I won't be home until in the morning. I have to perform an emergency appendectomy, and then I have to assist on the removal of cancerous lung tissue," Anthony explained from the other end of the phone.

"I understand. Good luck," I uttered in a detached tone. I was used to receiving such calls from my husband, though lately they had become more frequent.

After saying goodbye to Anthony, my mood was totally shot. I showered, drank a glass of wine, and hit the sack.

Prince had me on all fours giving it to me hard. He was so deep inside of me I could feel him in my stomach. "You're my wife now, don't hold back," he said in a deep seductive way.

"Okay, baby, how does this feel?" I asked, grinding back at him.

"Like paradise."

"I'm in paradise too. I love you so much," I whispered with my eyes closed enjoying every inch of him that went in and out of my wetness. My naked breasts were swinging back and forth from his strong pumps.

"I love you more," he let me know right above a whisper into the nape of my neck and pushed further inside of me.

"Baby, take it out a little, you're huge," I pleaded from the stinging sensation of his dick. It felt as if my vagina was going to be ripped apart. I was hurting, but at the same time I was enjoying the long strokes.

"You'll get used to it," he assured me and slowed his strokes down and made them gentle. He continued to glide in and out until we exploded together in sweet harmony.

I awoke early the next morning to find my panties off and sheets soiled. I removed my hand from between my thighs and headed to the shower feeling, oh so good.

Ca$h

Chapter 19
Solange

Shaheed's cell phone vibrated on the bed startling me from my sleep. I waited for him to roll over and answer it, but he was out for the count. I quietly reached for his mobile device, curious to know if it was a bitch blowing his number up.

"What you doing, shawdy?" he interrogated, catching me just when I was about to answer the call. "Nothing, baby. I was about to hand you your phone, that's all," I falsely answered, lying like a rug.

I handed him the phone and beamed my ears to his end of the conversation. He voiced a few commands then crawled out of bed and put his gear on.

"Where you 'bout to go?" I accusatorily questioned while placing my head back on my pillow, lying on my side facing him.

"That was Renogade. I gotta go handle something that's long overdue. I'll be back in an hour or so."

He was zipping up his jeans when I started being dramatic. "That's probably one of your hos calling you for some late night dick."

"Nawl, shawdy, I don't kick it like that. You know how I get down. Sometimes, I gotta get my hands dirty. I can't leave all the dirty work up to my nigga."

"Yeah…whateva!" I turned over on my other side and closed my eyes.

"Solange, why you so distrustful? I don't hide shit from you. I guess you don't trust me because your own closet is full of skeletons," he countered.

"Hmph! My closet is as clean as a whistle," I fired back.

"So you say. While I'm gone think of a good excuse for why I saw a used pregnancy test in your trash can. You couldna thought you was pregnant by me because I've always pulled out."

"That was my sister's EPT," I fibbed. I closed my eyes even tighter and hoped he'd buy that lie, I was trying to sell.

"And I'm the muthafuckin' Easter Bunny."

He left out without saying another word.

It was a couple of days before I saw or talked to him again. He showed up early in the morning wearing black Coogi jeans and a crisp white tee along with a fresh pair of MJ's on his feet. He was clutching a newspaper in his hand and sat down at the kitchen table watching me prepare breakfast in my pink baby tee and a white thong.

Asia was at school so we were alone.

"Fix me some breakfast, shawdy. While you're at it let me hear what lie you've made up about the pregnancy test," he grilled.

I was bent over at the stove and putting biscuits in the oven when I rose up, closed the oven's door, and looked over my shoulder. I sucked my teeth like...anywho! "Baby, what would you like to eat this morning?" I switched subjects because I wasn't in the mood for the bullshit he was on.

"A turkey omelet and some hash browns," he dryly announced.

"Dang. You must think I'm a chef."

"Stop playing. You know how to throw down. And I'm still waiting on that well-rehearsed lie."

I smacked my lips and placed a hand on my hip. "Boy, ain't nobody got to lie to you. Do you think that because you've always pulled out with me that I can't get pregnant? That doesn't always work. Ugh! You're acting like your elevator gets stuck trying to reach the top floor."

Shaheed shook his head and looked off. He let it go at that. Whether or not he was satisfied with my reply didn't even matter.

"Anyway, I'm not pregnant," I happily added.

I served him his plate then sat across from him at the kitchen table and poured myself a glass of orange juice to go with my slice of toasted raisin bread.

He slid the local section of the *Atlanta Journal-Constitution* to me and pointed to the headline of a story. *Man Found Dead From Gunshots To The Head* was printed in bold letters.

"Read the story and tell me if you know that bitch nigga," he instructed with a piece of egg hanging from his lip. He used his tongue to move the dangling food into his mouth.

My focus went from him to the news article which, I read in silence. When I was done all I could say was, "Good for his ass." I handed the article back to him, picked up my cup of OJ and made two swallows before placing the cup back on the table. I had no sympathy for Jamal. He got exactly what he deserved.

I concluded that the night Renegade called and Shaheed left my house in a hurry is when they caught Jamal's slimy ass and murked him.

"Oh well," I let out and crunched down on a bite of toast.

"Just remember, I go hard," boasted Shaheed and that shit made my juices flow like the Mississippi River. The fact that he handled someone that could've caused me to be in a casket with my eyes permanently shut, showed me how much this man truly cared about me. In my opinion, that was love.

Ca$h

Chapter 20
Prince

I stood in Lieutenant Wright's office and listened to her tell me all about my case.

"Damn, you all up in my business, ain't you?" I scoffed at her when she finished telling me. I sat in a chair across from her where she was browsing through her computer. Hot girl was wearing her uniform, but she was looking good as hell in it, ya heard me. But I acted like the shit didn't excite me. I didn't want her to think I was pussy riding like all the other lames on compound.

"I want to help you." She spoke with such sincerity that it broke through my defenses.

"Why?" I was confused to why she was so adamant about helping me out. She didn't owe me nothing.

"Because you once helped me," she replied without hesitation.

"You don't owe me for that."

"Maybe not, but I'd still like to help you regain your freedom. Reading over your trial transcripts it seems like you should have been acquitted. The verdict should have been justifiable homicide, but your attorney screwed things up."

"Yeah. I feel like he sold a nigga out."

"No, he was ineffective to the degree of causing the trial to be unfair," she said.

"Wait a minute. How do you know so much about litigation?" I asked and sat up straight in my chair interested in her response.

"I attended law school but ended up losing my passion for it."

"And you found your passion working in a prison?" I asked with a teaspoon of sarcasm.

"Of course not. This was supposed to have been sort of a temporary job for me, until I decided on a career. Somehow, I've been in corrections much longer than I'd anticipated."

"Four years, right?"

She looked away from her computer and smiled at me. Her eyebrows rose and she asked, "Yes, how did you know that?"

"You're checking me out; I'm checking you out."

She flirtatiously kissed the palm of her hand and blew me a kiss. "Fair enough, but you have to be very discreet. You know how inmates talk," she warned.

"Don't worry, Nicole, I won't get you in trouble with the warden."

"I'll just have to trust you."

"I'm not like most of the dudes in here. I don't run my mouth, and I'm not about no games. I'ma go ahead and admit that I've been thinking about you ever since you reminded me how we met. See, I believe that everything happens for a reason." I went ahead and let her know the real.

She seemed to be considering my words, then she asked, "If that's so, what is the reason we met that night?"

"You already know."

The sparkle in her eyes told me that we were on the same page. "Lieutenant," I went on to say.

She made a screw face at me which I took to mean that as long as we were alone she preferred that I called her by her name.

"Nicole," I corrected myself. "How far are you willing to go to really get to know a nigga and help me get my conviction reversed?"

"I won't be made a fool," she bluntly commented.

"I won't try to play you for one, but let me say this off the dribble. This place is like a fish bowl, dudes watch and see everything. I said that to say that you can't keep calling me to the office or some rumors will begin to spread like a germ. Niggas know that I'm not a snitch, so they'll easily guess that something personal is going down," I told her in a low tone.

"So what should we do? I enjoy seeing you every day."

"Assign me to the hall detail down here. I'll buff these crackers' floors if it will allow me to holla at you, but you have to fire white boy, Kilpatrick. He's already assigned to the hall detail; he's a known rat."

"I can do that," she agreed.

I knew that my next demand wouldn't be easy to get her to agree to. She was starry-eyed, but she looked like she was also a bit skeptical of my intentions. That was evident by her comment that she would not be made a fool of.

"One last thing, I need you to bring me a cell phone. Nothing expensive, just a cheap flip joint with a camera on it so we can talk and send each other pics," I dared and waited for her reaction.

"Prince, I don't know about that," she wavered.

"Aight, I'm not pressing you to do it. Just consider it, okay?" I removed myself from the chair, ready to push on out of there.

"I will. You need to consider not selling drugs around here."

I shrugged. "I gotta do what I gotta do, to get lawyer fees up. I told you my ex messed up all the money I left with her."

A knock on the door startled us both.

"Come in," Nicole answered in her most official tone.

In stepped Captain Lewis, her superior, and the epitome of an Uncle Tom. Captain Lewis had been working in corrections for twenty years and was much harder on his own race than he was on white boys.

"Is inmate Myers in some new trouble?" he asked like I was on some type of mischief.

"Not this time. I was warning him that if his name comes up in any type of inappropriate conduct that I won't hesitate to send him back to the hole," Nicole said to mislead the bastard.

"Cap', I'm thinking about assigning Myers to the lower hall detail where we can keep an eye on him. What do you think?" she asked, waiting for his approval.

"It might keep him out of trouble, though I doubt he's ever done any work in his life. Myers is a murderer and drug dealer," his slick ass tongue remarked.

I winked my eye at Nicole and left them alone to muddy my name. Nicole was slicker, than the picture she tried to portray. She would play right along with Captain Lewis while harboring much different feelings for me than she would let slip out in his presence.

A week later, I began working the lower hall detail which consisted mainly of keeping the long hallway outside of the lieutenant's office waxed and shining. Nicole had reassigned the white boy, Kilpatrick, to the kitchen detail to keep him out of our way.

"Don't tell me you're becoming a model inmate," joked Stack one day we were in the cell gettin' blunted out.

"Na, I'm still a convict. I'm just chillin' for a minute, while I try to get back in court and fight this life sentence." I kept the thing with Nicole to myself.

"You're doing the right thing," intoned Jabbo. "Too many young dudes come in here and lay down without tryna fight their convictions. They get caught up with the prison routine and give up on freedom. I respect that you haven't."

"I can't lay down, woady. I got a life out there. I got a daughter who needs me, and I can't do nothing for her in here." I coughed choking on the *loud* that me and Stack were smoking.

Fuckin' with Jabbo, I held the blunt out to him, knowing he didn't smoke. He reached for it, faking me out like he was going to accept it then snatched his hand back. I laughed. "Yo, Stack, it would be some funny shit to see Jabbo blazed, right? You know he already thinks he's a young jit. Let him hit this loud and he'll be walking around here sagging and busting raps."

Me and Stack cracked up. We took turns clowning Jabbo, but it was all done in fun and with respect, because, woady, was a triple OG whom we both had love for.

The next day Nicole brought me a prepaid cell phone. She'd smuggled it inside a condom and pushed it inside her vagina like I had coached her to do. Real talk, I smelled that condom repeatedly,

86

inhaling the sweet feminine scent that came from Nicole's inner walls. She smelled like candy, and I hated to have to flush that rubber down the toilet, but there was no sense in holding on to incriminating evidence.

I had already come up with a way to hide the cell phone in case of a shakedown. I made sure that the ringer was set for silent and that the phone's keyboard and main lights were programmed to remain on for seven seconds, the minimum amount of time. When making calls in the darkness of my cell, I didn't want a small bright light to be shining in case a C.O. happened to pass by.

About midnight the phone vibrated in my hand.

"Hello?" I answered in a whisper covering my head with a blanket. I knew that it was Nicole calling because she was the only one who knew my number. She had activated the phone and set up the phone's account in a fictitious name before bringing it to me.

"Hi. What are you doing?" Her voice was honey.

"Got my head covered with a blanket, thinking about you." I smirked. "Damn, you sound good."

"Thank you," she replied sounding nervous.

"Where's your husband?"

"He's still at the hospital. I did tell you that he works in the emergency room, didn't I?"

"Yeah, but let's not talk about him. Relax, Nicole, the feds aren't about to do a "kick door and run up in your spot and arrest you" for this. I promise you, I won't ever let this come back to hurt you. You're calling from the phone I told you to get for this purpose, aren't you?"

"Yes. The number can't be traced back to me."

"Good."

"Now, I've done my part, I expect for you to do yours," she said, alluding to the promise she had extracted from me to stop selling weed.

My silence must've spoken loud.

"Don't worry, Prince, I'm going to hire you an attorney, and I'll see to it that you have what you need in there. Just keep your promises, and I'll keep mine," she reiterated.

Because of shady bitches like Solange, it was difficult to trust what any woman said, but somehow Nicole broke down that wall. "I'ma do that," I heard myself say with sincerity.

Chapter 21
Solange

Shaheed was leaving out as my sister, Angie, was coming in with Asia in tow. Angie had picked Asia up from Mama's last night to stay at her house.

"How you doing?" I heard Shaheed speak to my sister whose only response was to turn her nose up at him.

Shaheed pushed on. When Angie was inside, I asked why she had to be so rude. She stood there looking at me as if the answer should have been obvious. She was geared in a red Michael Kors dress with a pair of Jimmy Choo pumps, and her long hair was in slightly tinted micro braids. My baby was wearing a new baby blue Ralph Lauren outfit that her auntie must've bought her. She jumped in my lap and got the sticky lollipop that she was sucking all over me.

"Get off me!" I yelled at her and slapped her across the leg. "Shut your mouth," I scolded when she began to wail like a brat.

"Do you have to be so mean to her?" Angie asked and let out a long sigh.

I looked at her sideways. "When you carry one inside of you for nine months, then you can discipline them however you choose to. Don't come at me like I abuse her." I shot her down.

"If you spent as much time with her as you do with those lowlife thugs that you like, maybe she wouldn't be craving so much attention. One would think that with Prince in prison and the dirt over Jamal not even hard yet, you would've had enough of street niggas."

"Maybe you should find yourself a man first, before you try telling me what type of niggas, I need to fuck with."

"No, sweetie, I don't need a man to be happy. It's called being independent and loving *yourself*."

"You know, the reason you're so uptight is because you don't get any dick. You need your pussy popped. Maybe you should go out and get yourself some thug lovin' and stop being so judgmental. Don't nobody wanna hear that shit," I lashed back from the sofa, looking up at her while we were tossing insults back and forth.

"Hmppff! It's a crime how you talk in front of Asia."

"And it's a felony how high up on a pedestal you try to put yourself. You make people not like you. Bitch, you still breathe the same air as the rest of us."

"I don't care who doesn't like me. As long as I'm able to pay my own bills and enjoy my three hundred thousand dollar home in the suburbs, I could give a rat's ass what you think of me."

"Bitch, you might be doing well financially, but you ain't got a man to cuddle with every night. You up in that big ass house fucking a dildo and shit." I hen cackled behind my own comment. The bitch was so prissy until it was pitiful as hell.

Angie stood over my head, getting all up in my personal space and blew up. "I'd rather play in my own stuff than let different men run up in me like a drive thru."

I hopped up, shoved her out of my face, and was about to tear into that ass when Asia started crying. "Hush, baby," I cooed.

Angie stormed out of the door and slammed it behind her.

I made Asia take off the clothes that Angie had bought her. "You don't need shit from that bitch," I said.

My cell phone rang as I was redressing Asia.

"Hello," I snapped, especially since I didn't recognize the number.

"Let me speak to Asia."

My pulse increased. It was Prince.

"Oh, hi baby daddy," I beamed. "How are you calling? I didn't hear a recording for a collect call." I removed the phone from my ear and looked at the number again to see if I could figure out where he was calling from. The number left me baffled so I pressed it back to my ear.

90

"Never mind that, put Asia on the phone." His tone smothered my excitement and left me feeling stupid.

"Nigga, if you don't want to talk to me, you can't talk to her."

"Don't nothing you do or say surprise me, Solange. It's all good, the rabbit will eventually hold the gun." The phone went dead in my ear.

I sat the cell phone on the end table and went outside to check my mailbox. There were three pieces of mail inside. My cable bill, my phone bill, and a letter from Prince addressed to...Mr. Sam!

My regular mail person was on vacation so the substitute carrier must have made the mistake. I carried the mail inside and hurriedly opened Mr. Sam's letter.

Mr. Sam,

I hope everything is going good with you, old man. As for myself, I'm trying to maintain and get back in court to fight this conviction. I can't even begin to imagine being in here for 30 years. Thanks for keeping me posted on all the drama going on with Solange, but you don't have to do that anymore. Whatever I once felt for her is gone now. As long as Asia is okay, I don't care to hear about anything else.

Take care and don't be chasing those young tails.

I couldn't believe what I had read. That old sneaky bastard!

"Asia, go in your room and play," I said, and then I raced next door and pounded on Mr. Sam's door. "Open up, you muthafucka!"

When he opened the door, I introduced his old, crusty face to my fist.

Ca$h

Chapter 22
Prince

Talking to Nicole for hours each night on the phone had a nigga drunk over her. We shared stories about our childhoods, discussed religion, politics, and parenting. I told her how things had really gone down the day I bodied the nigga and caught this charge.

"The nigga was all up in the club grabbing and talking stupid to Solange. I asked her where she knew the nigga from and she told me that she didn't know him. I told the fool to fall the fuck back. He swung a champagne bottle at my head; I ducked it and beat him down. It wasn't a problem, 'cause my hands are nice like that," I bragged.

"I bet they are." She laughed.

Continuing, I retold her how the same dude confronted me with a banger when the club was over. "I saw that he was drunk and since the situation was already, do or die, I reached for my own shit which was in my waist. So how did that make it murder because my trigger finger was quicker than his?"

"It should've been manslaughter at the most," she cosigned.

"That's what everybody says, but the DA had it in for me because I had beaten a murder rap a year earlier. I know my lawyer sold me out because later I learned that he and the DA had gone to law school together."

"Hmm. That's interesting," she said.

When we weren't discussing serious matters we talked about whatever came to mind. It seemed that her husband was seldom around.

I talked her into sending a couple of nude pics of herself to my phone and, on my dead ancestors, she had a body so flawless it seemed to have been air brushed by a professional artist.

I turned my CD player on in the background, and Kem helped me create a sensuous mood. "What are you wearing right now?" I asked as I pictured Nicole on the other end of the phone.

"My birthday suit," she disclosed. "Didn't you get the picture message I texted you?"

"Yeah, but I didn't know you took those just now."

"Of course. Who else would I have taken nude pictures for?"

"That's what's up," I remarked feeling like the boss I am. "Baby, I want you to close your eyes and imagine that I'm in bed with you. My tongue is caressing your nipples while my hands explore your body. Feel my strong touch rubbing your inner thighs. Play with your pussy like you'd want me to."

"Prince, I've never done this before," she shyly admitted.

"That's even better because I haven't either. We can do it together for the very first time," I said as I slid my hand inside my boxers. I laid on my back and fixed the pillow comfortably under my head ready to get it poppin' with this hot girl.

"Okay," she sweetly consented.

"You spoil a nigga, baby. Now rub that pussy for me. Make it real hot and wet, imagine this big dick up inside you."

"Oh my goodness, Prince. Your voice is making my pussy jump. This is crazy." I could hear her soft moans and groans escaping from her lips.

"Do you like to ride?"

"Umm, yes."

"Straddle me. Yeah, climb on top of this dick like that. Let every inch of me spread your walls and fill yo' wet pussy up. I'm gripping that round ass, lifting you up and down on this hard ass dick while you flick your tongue across your nipples. Your pussy is so wet and tight. I already want to bust a nut all up in that shit."

"Ohhh, keep talking to me."

"I'm making your pussy sloppy wet; it's gripping my dick tight tryna squeeze out my cum. But, I wanna make you cream all over it first. You wanna come for me, Nicole?"

"Oh yes, baby. Yesss! Oh, God! Oh Prince! I feel it about to come down. Oh, oh here it comes. Fuck me harder, baby. Oh lawddd!" cried out Nicole.

I stroked my dick faster until babies skeeted five feet across the room.

"I love you, Prince," said Nicole. "You don't have to say it back; I just wanted you to know how I feel."

The next day when I saw her, Lieutenant Wright was glowing like a 100-watt bulb. "That's what a thug will do to you," I teased in a low tone when she walked pass me in the hall.

"I'm not complaining, but I'm going to turn the thug into a man," she replied walking with extra sass in her steps.

A few months ago, I would've laughed at the thought of that, but now it seemed to be my destiny. Hustling wasn't even on my mind anymore.

Niggas on lock kept stepping to me about selling them some weed. When I told them that I was out of the game, they said that I was becoming rehabilitated. I knew that they were being sarcastic, but I just ignored them. One clown whispered that since I had a detail that put me around the staff I might be snitching on the low.

I caught ol' boy in the shower and left him with blood running down the drain. He didn't die, but he had to be airlifted by helicopter to an outside hospital.

"Ain't shit changed but my detail assignment," I reminded the whole cell block. You heard me!

Most niggas on lock were stuck on retarded and couldn't comprehend a nigga tossing down his criminal ways. It didn't matter to them that I was trying to chill, stay out of the bullshit, and get my conviction overturned. All they cared about was that their weed source had dried up. I didn't give a fuck what they felt. I had promised Nicole that I wouldn't hustle anymore and I planned to keep that promise.

She had kept hers. The lawyer that she retained to represent me on appeal had been to visit me twice. He hadn't made any promises but he did say that my chances for reversal were favorable.

The day after I shanked the nigga in the shower, Nicole did not come to work. When I called her that night I could tell that she was upset.

"You mad at me?" I asked.

"Yes, because what you did can get you more charges if someone tells. What if the man dies? How much sense does it make for us to fight one conviction while you constantly risk getting other serious charges?" she lectured.

"Well, if you're waiting for me to apologize for doing what a man in my situation has to do, you'll grow old before I do. Dude insinuated that I might be a snitch, ain't no pardon for that shit. I promised to chill and I have, but I'll never turn pussy. As much as I want my freedom back, I'll give up the chance to regain it before I allow a nigga to slander my name like he tried to do. If you can't understand that then you don't understand the man that I am."

I paused for a minute, but couldn't end it there because I still needed to kick some real shit to her. "If I ever get out of here and you and I get married, like we've talked about doing, I'm done with the streets, but if a fool kicked in our door, I'm not grabbing the phone and dialing 911. I'ma grab my glock and make his family dress him in a suit, ya heard me. I'm not looking for trouble, but I will deal with it if it comes my way." I made it clear to her.

"I just don't want you to get in anymore trouble," Nicole said caringly.

"Niggas better respect this shit, then," I stated.

Chapter 23
Solange

After taking my foot out of Mr. Sam's behind, I came back home, poured myself a drink, and sat down at the kitchen table thinking about all of my business that he had probably told Prince. Damn, my mind was blown.

Now I understood why Prince was so upset with me. All of this time I was lying to him to cover up my transgressions and Mr. Sam was going behind my back telling him the truth. *So that's how Prince knew about Jamal. I'll never get him back.*

Before long, I was crying in my cup. Asia came to the kitchen getting on my last damn nerve with all of her questions.

"What's wrong, Mommie?" she wanted to know.

"Nothing! Now go back in your room and stay out of my way before I beat you." I went off on her. I didn't say anything about her daddy not wanting me anymore; because Shaheed was in the bedroom watching television. It was up loud enough that it sounded like he thought he was at the movies somewhere. That was good because it stopped him from hearing me giving Mr. Sam the business.

The next day was no better. I was still in my feelings, but at least I got to take my frustrations out on a bitch.

I had gone to Wal-Mart to get a few movies hoping they would occupy Asia long enough for me to fucking breathe. On the way back to my car, who did I see parked three spaces away getting out of her Nissan Maxima?

Tash!

I hurried up and put Asia in the car, strapping her in her car seat. I closed the door and stalked up to my frenemy. 'Cause she was definitely a combination of a fake ass friend and enemy. "Bitch, you know you got to pay for that shit you did," I threatened, kicking off my heeled sandals.

"Honey, please, I ain't got time for your stupid ass today. Besides, I'm a diva. I don't fight in public," she tossed over her shoulder as she continued toward the store.

I followed behind her, itching for a piece of her smart black ass. "Oh, ho, you're not so bad without Renegade at your side, huh?"

I snatched her by the back of her weave and spun her around into my five friends. Blood ran from her busted lip. I mushed her face like she had done mine that night. She swung back, but her licks were too damn girly to go compete with mine. Tash wasn't a fighter, all throughout school I had to fight her battles. I warded off her blows with my forearm then socked her dead in the eye, trying to knock her contact lens out of her pupils. "You crossed the wrong bitch," I yelled and slammed my fist into her stomach.

Tash doubled over and fell to the ground. That's when the bottom of my shoe greeted her mouth.

Shaheed laughed. "Why you beat her down like that?" he asked. "Shawdy's 'round here looking like a raccoon by the eyes. She over at Renegade's crib with a big ass ice pack on her shit. Word, you a female Mayweather Junior."

"Hmmpff! I should've beat that bitch's ass into the middle of next week," I fumed. I was still mad at that ho.

It had been two days after the fact, and I was still sizzling. Shaheed thought it was funny.

"My nigga, Renegade, felt some kind of way about you kickin' Tash ass, but I told him he ought to teach his bitch how to fight," he cracked.

"It wouldn't matter. I would still bust that ass," I bragged.

Shaheed grinned and pulled me onto his lap. "That's why I fucks with you. I got myself a gangsta girl."

"And I got myself a real boss nigga," I returned the compliment, bending my neck and sliding my tongue inside his mouth.

Asia was in her bedroom asleep, so I didn't have to worry about her little cock blocking behind coming out and bursting up my groove. I slid down to my knees, unzipped him, and stepped to a bitch's business.

"Hold up, shawdy." He stopped me to remove the gun from his waist.

He sat it on the end table, and I resumed to giving him some face time. In less than five minutes, I was swallowing his sperm, licking my lips.

"Now stand up and let me taste that sweet pussy," he said, guiding me to my feet and lifting up the long t-shirt that I wore as a sleeping gown. He eased my thong to the side and slid his tongue up the length of my pussy while cupping my ass.

"Lick my clit," I begged.

He flicked his tongue back and forth across my pleasure button until it became as hard as a pebble. I spread my legs and guided his hands down to my wet opening. "Finger fuck me, baby."

My pussy squished as his thick fingers plunged deep inside of me. I came so hard my legs felt like noodles. He stood up, lifted me into his arms, and carried me into the bedroom. As soon as I caught my breath, I put the pussy on him as good as always. "Give me that cum, nigga. Give it here," I said followed by a moan while he fucked me from the back.

"Oh shit, I'm about to bust." He grunted then flooded me with his nut.

We laid there for a while, both of us panting. Then I nudged Shaheed. "You're heavy," I complained.

He rolled off me onto his back. "Baby Doll, you got that sho' nuff!" he exclaimed.

"Thank you, baby," I cooed, sliding down and taking his sticky bite-sized beef into my mouth. My juices tasted sweet on his thick little dick.

"Yeah, get that muthafucka back hard," he urged, placing both hands on the back of my head.

"Fuck my mouth, boo," I said in between slurps.

Just then, Asia came bursting into the bedroom. "Mama! Mama!"

"Oh, shit!" cried Shaheed, tryna pull his dick out of my mouth and cover himself.

Asia stood right there by the bed looking bewildered as hell.

"Well, she's already seen it now," I said continuing to stroke Shaheed. "She's gonna have to learn one day— might as well learn from the best."

I put his meat right back in my mouth.

"Hell no, shawdy! Get the fuck up!" snapped Shaheed, roughly pushing me away.

I kicked at Asia and hollered, "Take your ass outside and play!"

I didn't want Shaheed to think that I was an unfit mother so I said, "Baby, I'll be right back. Let me go make sure that Asia is good."

I pulled on some shorts and a top, stepped into some sandals, and then went outside to apologize to my baby. She was kicking a beach ball in front of the front yard. The ball rolled into the street, and she chased behind it. "No, Asia!" I screamed because a vehicle had just bent the corner on two wheels. It sped toward my baby!

She looked up just as the driver slammed on brakes and the car went into a long skid.

"Oh, my God!" I screamed.

Chapter 24
Nicole

It had been a long day at work, and I was not in the best of moods for several reasons. First of all, Prince had some words with Captain Lewis and the captain fired him from the lower hall detail.

"That was so stupid of you!" I muttered under my breath while escorting him back to the cell block.

"Shawdy, you ain't sayin' nothing. You didn't expect me to tap dance for that nigga, did you?" he'd blown me off.

"Now I won't get to see you every day!" I tensely whispered.

"It is what it is, ya heard me."

"Will you please stop saying that? Really, right now it's irritating." I wondered if my emotions were written across my face.

Prince chuckled. "I thought you loved that shit," he said and slapped me on the behind.

I hurriedly looked around to see if anyone had seen us.

"Don't do that!" I admonished him.

"Hush, that's mine."

I didn't see a damn thing funny. I whirled on my heels and went back to my office, hotter than a boiling pot. I was risking everything for him, and he was taking shit as a joke. Add to that, my cycle had just come on that morning before I left for work, so I was not in the mood for Prince's nonchalant attitude.

Now driving home from work, traffic was backed up. It took me forever and a day to reach my house, I was so looking forward to a shower and relaxation.

Anthony wasn't at home. I called his cell to ask what he wanted for dinner. Unfortunately, I was sent to voice mail. I figured that he was in surgery. I put on some sweats and a T-shirt, went into the kitchen, and searched the top of the drawer on the island for the recipe for a Cajun chicken dish that I wanted to try.

"I know I put it here," I said aloud. I hated when Anthony moved my things.

Slightly frustrated, I searched each drawer. In the bottom drawer I ran across a document that caused my mouth to fall to the floor. It was a bank statement in my husband's name from an account that I knew nothing about. The account had a balance of eighty thousand dollars! I felt my blood pressure soar to the ceiling.

I looked over the itemized report and saw payouts to expensive restaurants, hotels, spas, beauty salons—none of which I had ever patronized. Hundreds of dollars had been spent at Victoria's Secrets in the past month. I knew damn well that Anthony hadn't brought me any lingerie in almost six months. But all of that was nothing compared to the last four transactions on the statement. Mortgage payment on a condo that I knew nothing about. The purchase of a 2012 Lexus. Payments to a CVS drug store and to an OB-GYN on Northside Drive.

Tear drops tumbled down my face. I could not believe what was before my eyes. All that time he was saying that he was at the hospital, his deceitful ass had been caking some woman! In spite of my own secrets, I felt betrayed.

Numerous visits to the OB-GYN could only mean one thing— Anthony had fathered a child with another woman. I felt like such a fool.

Okay, calm down, I told myself. Wasn't I committing adultery with Prince? What made my actions less wrong than Anthony's? That was the reasonable way of viewing things, but that was bullshit. I had not fucked Prince. Oh yes, I wanted to but I hadn't.

On several occasions, the opportunity to duck off somewhere in the prison with Prince had presented itself. In fact, Prince had been pressuring me to do so. *"No, baby, I wouldn't feel right,"* I'd decline. *"Even when we had phone sex that once, I felt dirty. When we make love, I want to be divorced, and I don't want our first time to be in a filthy prison mop closet." I had stood firm against Prince's pressure.*

I wasn't excusing myself from all wrongdoings, but the extent that Anthony's infidelities reached far outweighed mine. A baby? A condo? A Lexus?

"I'm going to kill him," I cried to the walls.

I poured myself a glass of liquor, the hard shit that Anthony drank, the gin burned my throat as it went down. Thirty minutes and a glass and a half later, Anthony walked in the front door. "Baby, I'm home," he called out.

"I'm in the kitchen," I slurred.

I reached for the closest object to me as I heard his footsteps nearing. I was looking dazed when he entered the kitchen. I held the weapon in my hand; my teeth were bared, ready to attack.

"Nicole, what's wrong?" Anthony asked.

"You fucker!" I snarled, and then swung the large wooden spoon at his head.

"Aww!" he yelped when it cracked his crown.

I pummeled him as he tried to ward off my angry blows. By the time my arms grew weary, Anthony was on the floor in a ball, begging me not to hit him again.

"What are you talking about, honey?" he screeched.

I snatched the bank statement off the counter and shoved it in his face. "This!" I screamed, letting it fall in his lap.

He picked the pages up and looked them over familiarity and resignation. Realizing that he was busted, Anthony sat up and took a deep breath. Then he exhaled and muttered, "She's seven months."

"When were you planning on telling me?"

"After Amber had the baby," he dropped his head and admitted.

Amber? I dropped the spoon, stepping a few steps back. The shock of his disclosure sobered me. "Isn't that the intern you trained last summer?" I needlessly questioned. My recall was flawless. Amber was a Christina Milian looking heifer that he had invited to our house for dinner several times.

"I'm sorry, it was an accident." His weak excuse infuriated me.

"An accident, Anthony? This same woman sat at our dinner table. Just weeks ago when I had lunch with you at the hospital, I rubbed her swollen belly. She had invited me to her baby shower. How dare you two make a fool of me!"

Anthony climbed to his feet, waiting for my temper to subside. I went on another five minutes thinking back on the many occasions on which he and Amber smiled in my face while stabbing me in the back. My voice was hoarse when I stopped screaming at him.

"Nicole, I'll give you a divorce. That's the best thing because I'm not in love with you anymore," he was brave enough to say.

Whap! I slapped the shit out of his cheek.

A short while later, I was crying on Raven's pillow. "You know, it's not so much the cheating that hurts. It's not even that he chose to do it with *her*. It's the baby thing," I confessed while I wept.

"I know, gurl." My best friend understood.

She knew that I had been unable to get pregnant. Anthony and I had consulted with several well-regarded fertility specialists; it was their conclusion that my hormones were imbalanced. Therefore, I was told that I might not ever conceive. As a woman, that led to feelings of inadequacy. Anthony had once joked, "At least we don't need condoms."

I had giggled. Later, I had gone into the bathroom and cried. Recounting it to Raven now, I sobbed. She held me in her arms until I felt better.

"You're such a friend," I thanked her.

"So are you," she kindly replied.

One of my phones rang. Raven picked it up.

"No, I have nothing to say to him!"

I shook my head when she tried to pass me the phone.

"It's Prince," she said, handing me the phone that I had bought particularly for his calls.

I accepted it.

"Hey, Beautiful." Prince's voice was exactly what I needed to hear.

Ca$h

Chapter 25
Prince

Shorty was all fucked up in the head and her pain felt like my own. I wanted to escape from prison and go handle her husband. She may have rocked his last name for the time being, but in our hearts she was *my* girl.

I hadn't really known that I loved Nicole until I heard her tears on the phone that night. That shit threw me off. "Don't cry, baby. I love you," I told her.

My words may have comforted her some but apparently not enough because she didn't come to work for the next three days. We had spoken on the phone each day though.

Finally, her spirits were uplifted and she returned to work on the fourth day. As soon as I found out she was back I decided to go see her.

"Say, C.O., I need a pass to go see Lieutenant Wright. She confiscated my CD player last week, and she's supposed to give it back to me today." I ran game on the young, white boy who was working the cell block. He was fresh out of training and scared to death of all of us cock diesel niggas on lock.

With pass in hand, I made it to Nicole's office without being harassed by any of the officers I had to pass by on the way. Her door was closed, but I could see her through the door's large window. She sat behind her desk looking fly as hell, but her expression was sad.

I knocked on the door.

"Come in," she answered, looking up from her work.

"Sup now?" I closed the door behind me and sat down facing her with the desk between us and my back to the door.

"Hi. How did you get down here?" she asked twirling an ink pen between her thumb and forefinger. Her nails were a rainbow of colors.

"I gamed a new jack into writing me a pass. You know I had to come check on my girl."

Nicole smiled weakly. Her eyes still showed evidence of the many tears she had shed the past days. I stared into those tired eyes and spoke from the heart. I said, "Shawdy, that nigga didn't deserve you. Any man worth his weight would know that you're the type of woman to hold on to. Besides, baby, you wasn't happy no way. I believe that there's only one right person for us in the world. Anyone else is only a substitute. Now, whether we ever meet that person is the thing. But in us, you and me, we've met that one person who was meant for us. So, do your best to put what happened behind you."

"I will," she promised. Then she lifted her hand so that I could see that she was no longer rockin' her wedding ring. "Ya heard me," she joked.

I smiled at her and she returned the smile.

"Everything is gon' be okay," I reassured her.

"Thank you," she replied.

"Well, I'ma head back to the cell block, it's almost count time," I said.

I saw a light flash in Nicole's eyes. "No, you can stay. I'm going to place you on the out count." She smiled at me mischievously, then placed a call to my block and told the officer that I was logged on her out count. That meant that we would have about twenty minutes alone while the rest of the prison was locked down for count.

"What's on your mind?" I asked, already knowing the answer.

Chapter 26
Nicole

For a moment, we just sat there staring at each other. Then Prince licked his lips, and I did the same. "Hold up, let me check the hallway," he said.

My heart pounded. Fear and excitement had me short of breath. Coming back into the office, Prince closed the door then turned back around to face me. "It's all good," he declared. "Can I have you like I want to?"

"Yes, baby."

He unbuckled his pants, then came around the desk, reached for my hand, and led me into a corner of the office where we would be blocked by a file cabinet. "I'm scared," I said as he pulled me against the bulge in his pants.

"We're good." He stepped back and dropped his pants. What I saw sticking out of his boxers caused me to suck in my breath. It was huge! Ten inches with thick veins!

"Prince, maybe we…"

"Relax, baby girl."

He grabbed my hand and placed it around his thickness. My knees almost betrayed me. He covered my mouth with his, simultaneously unbuckling my pants and gently stroking my folds.

"My lord!" I whispered.

"Na, *your nigga,*" he corrected and his finger rubbed.

At the same time, my hand slid up and down the length of him. His width could not be encircled. "Hurry, put it in," I moaned.

He lifted one of my legs up while allowing me to brace my back against the wall. I was on that ride to Heaven when he entered my vajay-jay.

"Oooh baby, you feel so good," he whispered into my neck.

"Hurry, Prince." I was afraid of being caught.

"Nah love, I'm not hurrying. We're about to enjoy this opportunity."

He moved in and out of me with long gentle strokes. My head fell back and my legs quivered. His dick filled me up completely, and had I not been slippery wet there would've been no room left for him to slide in and out.

"Oh, baby," I moaned as I matched his rhythm.

"Shit! You feel so damn good." He sucked in his breath and started stroking faster. The friction down low set me on fire.

My vision became blurry. "Ahhhh! I bit down on his shoulder as my love flowed down like a stream.

Prince exploded inside me seconds after my juices coated his big juicy dick. "Arghhhh!" He growled ina low guttural tone.

"Get dressed!" I hurried him.

"We good, baby," he replied, cool as can be.

Chapter 27
Solange

I sat in the emergency room of Eglestor's Children Hospital crying hysterically. The paramedics had allowed me to ride in the back of the emergency van that whisked Asia to the hospital after she was struck by the car. I had prayed the whole ride there, promising God that I would be a better mother to my daughter if He would bring us through this without Asia being seriously injured.

Shaheed arrived, and I rushed into his arms.

"It's all my fault," I wept.

"No, shawdy, don't blame yourself."

"I have to because I shouldn't have yelled at her." My head rested against his chest and my tears soaked his shirt.

"Shhh. It'll be okay," he comforted.

I looked up and saw Mama and Angie flying toward us. Shaheed released me, and I ran into Mama's arms. "My baby," I cried.

Mama stroked my hair like she'd done when I was a little girl. "Have you heard anything about her condition?" she gently asked.

"No, ma'am. The doctor is supposed to come out and speak with me shortly."

Angie leaned in and made it a group hug. "She's going to be alright, lil' sis. I've been praying for her."

My sister's compassion was touching, considering our recent riff. "Thank you." I sniffled back more tears.

Mama looked up at Shaheed, her eyes scoured every inch of him. I could tell that she disapproved of him instantly. "Who is he?" she asked in a tone that was as offensive as her look.

"I'm sorry," I apologized. Then I made the proper introductions all around.

Angie smiled at Shaheed while Mama sneered, mumbling, "Just another thug." I shot her a dirty look.

"Don't pay her no mind," I whispered to Shaheed.

Looking over Shaheed's shoulder, I noticed Mr. Sam approaching. He was wearing a dingy white T-shirt under a pair of blue jean overalls. *Just country as hell!* I was about to give his old ass a real reason to be in the emergency room. *This old goat has some nerves!* I steamed before reminding myself that his concern for Asia outweighed his snitching on me to Prince. Still, I rolled my eyes at him.

Mama warmly greeted him; they had always been flirty with each other. In fact, Mr. Sam kept up Mama's yard. "How's the little angel doing?" I overheard him ask mama.

"We haven't heard anything yet," Mama replied, solemnly, as she and Mr. Sam sat down, side by side. Angie winked her eye at me but, I didn't know why.

To my relief, a tall white man wearing green surgical scrubs approached our group. My nerves were so jittery I could barely breathe. "Are you the family of Asia Myers?" he asked.

"Yes, I'm her mother," I managed to say, although my mouth was dry as cotton. I tried to read his expression, but it gave no clue as to how my baby was doing. "Doctor, how is she?" I asked as I folded my arms and hoped he'd give me a good report.

"She's fine, considering," he said, and I let out a long sigh and silently thanked the Creator. "She did suffer a fractured collarbone and a broken fibula."

Streams of water rolled down my cheeks. I didn't know what I would have done if it had been worse. The doctor went on to explain each of Asia's injuries, scrapes, and bruises. I listened, but I was just relieved to hear that none of her injuries was severe and that she would be released from the hospital in two days.

"Thank you, Jesus!" I let out. I added, "Uh…and you too doctor." He gave me a nod and a pat on the back before stepping away and going back down the hall.

Asia smiled so big when we opened the door to her bedroom, and she saw balloons, teddy bears, and "get well" streamers decorating the room. Shaheed was pushing her in a wheelchair; he had been with me and by my side through the whole ordeal.

I had overheard whispers of several of his phone conversations the past day or two— some type of beef was going on with him and Renegade— but he set it aside to remain at the hospital with me until my baby was released. That earned him my heart.

Asia's medication made her eyes slowly shut, putting her to sleep. She was probably dreaming about the fluffy white poodle that Shaheed promised to buy her once she recovered. "You've been so caring and supportive throughout all of this," I acknowledged with sincere appreciation. Thank you so much, baby." I placed my arms around his neck while he held me around my waist and planted a wet kiss on my neck.

"It's nothing, shawdy," he humbly replied. He released me. I sat on the edge of my bed and used his fingertips to massage my shoulders and neck trying to massage away the stress that I was feeling.

I leaned back and relaxed my shoulders, caught up in the moment. I contemplated whether I should've contacted Prince and told him what happened to Asia. He had the right to know, but I feared he would come at me like I was an unfit mother. I didn't want to fight with him on that issue.

I thought back to earlier in the day, before the accident, when Asia had burst into the bedroom while I was giving Shaheed some head. *God forgive me,* I said, recalling my mean remarks. I really needed to change my life. I needed to be a better woman and a better mother to my daughter.

I felt the soothing massage deep in my muscles. Shaheed not only made me feel good, he was good for me. He had shown that he cared more for me and my daughter than I had thought. I could actually see myself settling down. *Damn, did a bitch just say that?* I thought to myself with a smile.

Though I was only twenty-six years old, I had been through a lot. Most of the bullshit that I had been through involved trife niggas. Their doggish ways had turned me into the conniving chick that I was before I met Prince. Once Prince got locked up, the old me resurfaced, but I was truly tired of that shit. Fucking different men, playing them out of their pockets for money— it was so old.

I wanted to let my guards down and allow myself to love and to be loved by Shaheed. It was scary because that would mean I would have to completely stop loving Prince. What made my decision less difficult was the fact that I knew that Prince would never forgive me for sleeping with Jamal. In addition to that, Prince was in prison for life—I needed someone who could be with me now.

"What's on your mind, baby doll?" Shaheed asked reading me like an open letter.

I sighed. "Just life in general, and us in particular."

"I'm listening," he prompted.

It was only natural for me to consider lying; that had been my most trusted defense mechanism for years. Painful experiences had taught me not to trust any man with my heart or the truth. Because once you gave them either, they would shit on you. The thought of being completely honest with Shaheed about my feelings was comparable to standing at the edge of a mountain and looking down, trusting the wind to hold me up if I jumped. A bitch was terrified! Yet, I decided to take a leap.

"Baby, I'm just thinking about how hard it is to give you my all. I know that you care about me—you proved that—but I've been used and abused so much by men."

I stopped there and became emotional.

Shaheed wrapped his arms around me. Softly he said, "Solange, it's okay to talk about it. I love you, and nothin' you tell me will change that."

"Are you sure?"

"Yes, baby."

114

I broke down in his arms, pouring out my heart, and revealing my deepest secrets. I told him about being molested by my stepfather. "When Mama found out and left him, I blamed myself for her struggling to keep a roof over our heads since our provider was gone," I cried.

"For a while I had to go live with my grandmother in Mississippi. While there, my uncle raped me. I was only twelve years old at the time, and he was in his thirties. I've never told anyone about it until now." I sobbed on his shoulder as I recalled the incident.

"Where the nigga at now?" Shaheed asked in a hostile manner.

"He's dead. He got killed in an accident at his job."

"Shoulda got shot in the muthafuckin' head."

"After my uncle raped me, I began sleeping with all the boys in the neighborhood. Granny sent me back to Atlanta, but that didn't end my promiscuousness. My stepfather and uncle made me feel like a ho, so I acted like one."

"You wasn't no ho, shawdy. You was an abused child," he correctly interpreted.

I cried while he embraced me for a long time. Shaheed held me in his arms and didn't utter a word. In the morning, he awoke me with a kiss.

"Today is a new day, baby," he tenderly said. "Nothing about the past matters, okay?"

"Yes," I agreed.

"I want you to be my wife."

"And I wanna be," I heard myself respond.

"Good. Now, I want you to go visit your baby daddy and tell him the deal. That's what I would want you to do if I was in his shoes. A man will always respect the truth even if he doesn't like it."

I nodded in agreement, adding, "Baby, I have some money of his. He thinks someone stole it from me, but I want to tell him the truth and give it back to him. What do you think about that?"

"The money I had, right?" asked Shaheed.

"Yeah, the ninety stacks, but I feel me and Asia are entitled to half."

"Nawl, shorty, that man is locked up. Give him all of it back. I got you and Asia."

That was so touching, but I wasn't giving Prince back all of shit.

Chapter 28
Nicole

In the weeks following our first intimate contact, Prince and I became even closer than we had been before. We hadn't had sex again, but that one time seemed to sustain me until we could be together for real.

I had filed for divorce from Anthony, and he had smartly agreed to a cash settlement that was fair. I could have taken him to the cleaners because his infidelities were out in the open while mine remained a secret. However, all I wanted was to be out of the marriage and free to love Prince without guilt.

"I'm going to use most of the money from my divorce settlement to pay the attorneys that I've hired to handle your appeal, baby. Just stay out of trouble. The attorneys have already reviewed your trial transcripts and they're very optimistic." I passed on to him what the lawyers related to me. We were on the phone in the middle of the night.

"Okay. Now, can we break in your new apartment?" he asked.

"We sure can. I'm already touching myself."

Prince had turned me into his little phone sex fiend.

"You got your panties off?"

"I don't wear panties to bed."

"Um...that shit just made my dick jump."

"Let it jump right inside of me," I seductively offered.

"Hell yeah. I wanna get real deep tonight. I wanna make you feel like you felt when we were in your office. Baby, your pussy felt so tight and wet. It gripped this big ass dick like it didn't ever wanna let go." His voice was so husky I could picture him stroking himself. He continued talking, until we both were adding on the sexual fantasy that our next time would be. Lord, it seemed so real!

My pussy was so wet the juices ran down between my butt. "Prince, I'm so hot baby. Put out this fire." I let out a moan in his ear.

"Okay, baby. Come on this big dick. Cream all up and down it."

"Keep talking, baby."

"Nut all up on my dick."

"Ooh wee!"

"Give it to me."

"Ooh."

"Squeeze this dick with that wet pussy."

"Sssss!"

"Come for me, baby."

"Oooh, cum—with—me."

"I'ma come with you, baby."

"Cum, Prince. I—can't—hold—it."

Seconds later, we both erupted.

"Whew! My legs are shaking and my hair feels like a wet mop." I huffed trying to catch my breath and my clit was still jumping. I wondered if I wasn't turning into a nympho."

"Na, we just have the chemistry." He laughed when I voiced my concern.

Later, after I had showered and called him back, Prince gave me Solange's address and asked me to go check on his daughter. I eagerly agreed to do so; I just hoped that I wouldn't get into it with Solange. From the stories Prince told, I knew that Solange could be very extra.

Chapter 29
Solange

I felt so good after opening up to Shaheed. Damn, a bitch was in love! Shaheed, Asia, and I were in bed watching the cartoon, Jessie, on my plasma television.

My cell phone rang, disturbing the moment. I picked it up off the bed, frowning as I saw the caller's name. "Bitch, what you calling my phone for?" I blasted.

Tash meekly said, "I heard about the accident and even though we're beefing, Asia is still my god daughter."

"And?"

"Look, Solange, I don't want to…"

I cut off whatever it was she was going to say. "Bitch," I spat. "You shouldn't wanna do shit but stay the fuck out of my face! You already showed me how you get down. I guess you forgot that I'm the bitch who has had your back since we were kids."

I got up and walked out of the bedroom so that Asia wouldn't hear me cussing like a ho on the stroll.

"Trick, you sold me out for a nigga that cheats on you and slings dick around town like a food stamp card! Where was Renegade when your broke ass didn't have nowhere to stay? I let you live here until you got straight. When those bitches from Bankhead jumped your sorry ass, who went back with you and tore their asses up?" I continued on.

"You did," she forced herself to dryly admit.

"Damn right, I did! But you was gonna sit there and let Renegade kill me, bitch!"

"I'm sorry," she tried to apologize.

"You're right about that! You are damn sure one sorry, lowdown bitch. Call my number again and you better know karate the next time I see your ass!" I hung up on that dirty ho.

When I returned to the bedroom, Shaheed correctly guessed who I had been tongue boxing with. "I don't see why you spazzin', y'all gon' be back friends again," he predicted.

"Shaheed, don't play with me!" I scowled.

"Whatever, girl. Can a nigga get you to run to the store and get me a box of Black-n-Mild?"

"Yes, boo," I slowly agreed. It was nothing; he was being so sweet to me, it was the least I could do. "Let me drive your car."

I quickly threw on some clothes, left out and hopped in Shaheed's Dodge Challenger. Lil' Wayne's mixtape lyrics, 'No Worries'—blasted out the system as I whipped into the B.P. gas station around the corner from my house. I bought my boo two boxes of Black-n-Mild cigars and grabbed Asia some goodies. Coming out of the store I was approached by a tall, dark skinned dude rockin' dreads and Gucci'd down from head to toe. His platinum chain and key medallion hung down to his waist. And the nigga smelled ooh so good.

"Sup, ma?" His accent was New York, baby. I loved up North niggas.

"Hello," I replied, allowing my eyes to travel down to his dick print.

"Can I do the same to you?" he boldly asked, busting me out.

I almost said, *"yeah"* just out of habit. You know, always keep a backup. Then I realized that this was a test. If I couldn't turn down this thuglicious nigga, that meant I was still the same bitch.

"I'm sorry, boo. I'm involved with someone," I forced myself to say.

He nodded his understanding. Then he respectfully said, "It's all good, ma. Nice running into you anyway." He aimed his remote on his key ring and chirped the alarm.

This muthafucka is pushin' a Maybach! I was shocked. *Shaheed, I'ma fuck you up if you do me wrong,* I said to myself. *A bitch just turned down a nigga with major cake for your ass.*

Back on my street, I noticed a silver Mercedes Benz C-Class/C350 parked in front of Mr. Sam's house. A red bone chick with long flowing hair and a body to envy got out of the unfamiliar whip. I had never seen the chick before, but I knew Mr. Sam wasn't caking like that. Two pretty bitches can't share the same space, so I was instantly alarmed.

Who the fuck is she? I wondered.

Ca$h

Chapter 30
Nicole

I used my GPS to find the address that Prince gave me. I noticed a red Charger pull up in the driveway next door a few minutes after I parked at the curb of Mr. Sam's house. Something told me that the bright-skinned girl in the Charger was Solange. She was pretty, so I could see why Prince would have been attracted to her.

I marched up on Mr. Sam's porch and knocked on the door. I did not have to wait long for him to answer. When he opened the door, I saw that he fit the description Prince had given me of him. He was bald headed and clean-shaven with friendly eyes and a welcoming smile.

"May I help you?" he politely asked.

I told him who I was and that Prince had sent me to ask about Asia. I saw that the question bothered him. "She's okay, isn't she?" I asked, alarmed.

He invited me inside, but I declined his offer because the way he stared at my breast made me a little uncomfortable. Standing in his doorway, I listened in shock as he told me that Asia had been hit by a car. I was relieved to hear that Prince's daughter was okay, but sad that she had suffered a fractured collarbone and a broken leg.

"Well, I'm going to go over and see how she's doing," I decided.

"Oh no! You might not wanna do that—that Solange is some kinda crazy when she wants to be. She's quick to fight," he warned.

"I'm not afraid." I didn't expect a rumble, but I knew that I could hold my own if one broke out.

I marched across the yard and called out to Solange as she was getting out of the car. I figured she had sat there watching me the whole time I was talking to Mr. Sam because she had ample time to go inside had she wanted to. Hearing her name, she turned toward me as I approached.

Up close, we eyed each other. She was cute, but I wasn't intimidated. "Hi, I'm Nicole. I'm Prince's girlfriend. He asked me to come by to check on Asia," I conveyed and folded my arms waiting for a response.

Her lip instantly curled up and she began rolling her neck like a tidal wave. The girl surely had some serious issues.

"Well, I don't know why he sent you over here to check on my muthafuckin' daughter, but you needs to be steppin' before I send you back to wherever you came from on a stretcher," she threatened and tossed a plastic bag on the ground. A bag of Skittles and a pack of Black and Mild flew from the inside of the bag and landed on the ground. She removed her earrings and tossed them on top of the bag.

My eyes widened. I was appalled, but not afraid. I knew that with chicks like Solange, you had to stand up to them or they would clown you. I said, "I didn't come here to fight, but I don't know how to run so how are you carrying it?" She seemed shocked by my response, but she kept on with the drama that Prince had warned me she was about.

"Bitch, you feel froggish, leap," she encouraged with her fist balled as she bounced around me like she was on a trampoline. I swear she must've thought she was related to Money Mayweather.

"Oh no, honey, I never start a fight, I just win them." I unfolded my arms just in case she wanted to throw down. I really didn't have any intentions on arguing with her ignorant behind, but I wasn't about to let her touch me. I could've popped her first when she was taking off her earrings earlier, but I didn't want to steal on her. I kicked off my wedges, balled up my fist, and rubbed the tip of my nose with my thumb.

Let's do this!

She threw the first punch, and it landed on my cheek. The blow hit me so hard that my neck twisted from the power behind it. I should've known the ghetto looking broad could throw down, but it was all good. I grew up in the projects, which was something I never liked to mention. Hmph, all cakes taste the same. It's the icing that gives it a different flavor. Meaning don't let the prissy look trick you, I will get down just like the next broad when provoked.

I rapped her with a left hook and then a right. My birthstone ring collided with her eye. I grabbed her by her weave that dangled down her back and started putting in work. I used her hair to toss her around and beat her like she was a punching bag. She tripped over a stone that decorated her flower garden, and I dove right on top of her giving her a few more blows to the face.

Yeah, I was giving her what she asked for, and what made me even madder was the fact that she made me dirty up my faded Escada jeans. I banged her head on the ground three times when some guy and Mr. Sam tried to pry us apart. That's when she grabbed a fistful of my hair and got a chance to get a few licks off my skull. It seemed it took forever for them to pry her hands from my hair. I popped her one more time in the mouth before I was thrown damn near across the street by the guy.

The younger guy helped her off the ground and was holding her back. "Let me go, Shaheed. That bitch busted my nose!" screamed Solange, trying her best to charge at me. Cherry red blood oozed from her nose down onto her pink baby tee. Her blue jean Capris were full of dirt from me beating her down in that flowerbed. A yellow marigold flower was tangled up in her weave, and I actually wanted to laugh at her.

"Chill, shawdy," he said holding her in a tight grip with his arms around her waist.

I rubbed my eye when I felt a stinging sensation shooting through it. It was swelling, but I didn't care. Although I carried myself like a lady, I wanted her to know I wasn't a punk.

Later, I sat in Raven's kitchen with an ice pack on my swollen eye telling her all about the altercation with Prince's crazy ass baby mama. "Gurl, you have to love that man to go through all of this," she said as she sat at the bar stool cupping her chin up with her hand looking at my eye and shaking her head.

"I can't blame Prince for the way Solange acted. Really, I'm more concerned with how he will feel when I tell him about Asia's accident. He already feels bad that he's not out here to help raise her."

"I hear you, Nicole. I just hope he doesn't disappoint you. You know, you hear so many stories about men in prison making all those fake promises to women. Then, once they get out, they go the other way," Raven said.

"That's not who Prince is," I made known, instantly defending my man, because I believed in him whole-heartedly. I didn't care how many other men in prison lied to women. My heart told me that my man was different.

The next day, I went to work with a long red bruise under my black eye. I looked horrible, and I could only imagine how Solange was looking after the hurting I put on her behind.

I'm sure everyone probably thought that Anthony had put his hands on me. I told my supervisor that I had gotten hit in the eye with a tennis ball while playing with my best friend on the court. Ha! I didn't even know how to play tennis.

Prince saw me by the chow hall. I was overseeing chow call for E-block that day. "Lieutenant, I need to speak with you about getting some new sheets," he said.

"Okay, Myers. Wait by the door, and I'll talk to you after everyone is back in the dorm." I followed his lead.

After the hall was clear he asked, "Baby, what happened?" Then he guessed, "Anthony? I'ma fuck that nigga up!"

I found it cute that he wanted to defend me, but his anger was misplaced. I told him, "Anthony didn't do this. I got into a scrap with Solange when I went by there to check on Asia."

"What?" His eyebrows shot up.

126

"Uh, huh. I don't want to have to scrap with your baby's mother every time I see her somewhere. So I'm going to need you to get that situation under control," I demanded of him, keeping my voice low as possible.

"I'ma handle it, ya heard me."

"Please do," I insisted. I was not going to lower myself to hood rat status for the sake of love again.

Prince correctly interpreted my tone. "I said I'ma handle it," he repeated. "Did you find out how my daughter is doing?" he asked leaning against the cell block door with one hand. I gave him my report, and his whole expression changed. His eyes became hardened.

"She let my daughter get struck by a car?" he uttered shaking his head and frowning. "That rat bitch."

I did not disagree. In fact, I made sure that I added, "And she had some guy there when it happened."

Prince looked at me for a second, and I could see his eyes watering. "I gotta get out of here and get my shortie from that bitch."

"Yes you do, baby," I agreed.

"When I win that appeal and bounce up out of here we gon' make some Prince Juniors, okay?"

My response got stuck in my throat. How could I tell him that if he chose me there would be no babies? I wanted to tell him, but I was afraid I would lose him like I had Anthony. "You're so crazy." I forced a laugh. It was the best that I could come up with at the moment. No man wanted a woman, regardless of how beautiful she is, who couldn't conceive children in my opinion. I felt so worthless inside.

"Crazy about your pretty red ass," he remarked.

Will you feel the same once you find out that I can't give you kids? I wondered.

Changing the subject, I said, "I'm meeting with your attorneys again after work. They think that they've found something in your trial transcripts that will get your conviction reversed."

"Are you serious," he asked, getting excited.

"Of course. But try not to get too amped up in case it turns out to be groundless."

"I'ma be good either way. If this appeal shit don't work, I'm making fence parole."

I fired him a reproachful look. "What type of life would we have together on the run, Prince?" I squinted my eyes and waited to hear how he would answer. He sounded crazy as hell.

He shrugged. "Better than this," he countered, and I could not say a word.

"Cheer up, shawdy, it will all work out. Now let me go back inside before I get tempted to press your back up against that wall and take you to another galaxy."

I shot him the finger. "You are so arrogant," I said, but I was only kidding. I turned and walked away making my booty bounce just to tease his cocky butt.

I didn't have to turn around to know that he was checking me out, smiling at the fact that I was all his.

On the outside, I was wearing a smile as bright as his, but inside I was crying. I wasn't sure how to tell him that I was incapable of giving him a baby.

Chapter 31
Solange

Two days after getting into it with Prince's new bitch, I stood in the bedroom mirror examining my bruises. The knot on my forehead still throbbed, my nose still hurt, and my whole body was sore. How in the fuck did I let that prissy looking cow get the best of me?

"The next time I see her I'ma go right in that jaw," I blurted.

Shaheed got out of bed, came up from behind and wrapped his arms around me. He kissed my bare shoulder and advised, "Baby, you gotta learn to let shit go. You're too pretty to be throwin' down like some ghetto broad. Then, when you get into it with your baby's daddy's girl, it makes me wonder if you're still in love with him."

I didn't hesitate to assure him that he was so wrong. "I popped that bitch in the mouth because she had no business coming over here asking me shit about my child. And I should go next door and put my foot in Mr. Sam's old ass again. Every time I turn around, his old decrepit ass is all up in my business. I bet he ain't told nobody that he was throwing hints at a bitch!"

"Baby, fuck all that drama. Don't allow muthafuckas to knock you off your square. You know how many times muthafuckas blow me out in these streets. What if I blasted every nigga that rubbed me the wrong way? Shit would be like Baghdad around this bitch."

Shaheed was making sense, but I didn't wanna hear no fuckin' speech.

"I'm telling you, boo— a bitch about to snap if muthafuckas don't quit trying me!" I loudly vented.

He laughed to smother my anger.

"Ain't nothing funny." I smiled.

I waited until Shaheed hit the streets before I started marching over to Mr. Sam's. I noticed that his vehicle wasn't there. Luckily for that ass, he wasn't home. Lately his old ass had been away a whole lot. *I'll deal with his half dead ass another day,* I promised myself as I returned to my house.

A while later I was in Asia's room watching Dora with her on television when Mama called me on the house phone. "Hey, Ma, what's up?" I answered, knowing it would annoy her.

"Ain't shit up! Talk to me like I'm your mother and not one of your friends," she started. I muffled a giggle with my hand.

"Okay, how are you doing, Mother Dear?" I corrected.

"I'm fine. Does that man I saw you with at the hospital live with you?" she asked me. I wasn't expecting that question.

"Huh?"

"Don't huh me. Does he live with you or not?" She repeated the question and her voice was deeper the second time around.

"No, Ma, he has his own place but if he did, so what? I'm grown, need I remind you?"

"You may be grown, but that doesn't give you the right to do anything that you please. You don't know anything about that man to have him laying up in your damn house around my granddaughter," she fussed.

"Mama, please," I begged of her. "Anyway, I'm glad that you called."

"I don't know why. I don't have any money, if that's your next question."

I rolled my eyes and tossed up my finger, even though she couldn't see it and thank the Lord she couldn't. She was really working on my nerves. "Goodness, Ma! I'm not going to ask you for no money, dag. All I need is for you to keep Asia for me tomorrow while I go visit Prince. With that cast on her leg and her arm in that thingy, I don't want her to ride with me. The drive is too long."

"I'll keep her, but bring her by in the morning because I'm going to a church function this evening."

"Okay. Thank you, Ma," I sang with a big grin.

Shaheed didn't come back that day. I blew his phone up until he sent a text telling me that he was making a quick trip out of town to re-up on some product. I forced myself to believe him but it was hard because men are so sneaky.

In the morning, I woke up about 5 am and called Mama to prepare her for me dropping Asia off. I called and called but got no answer. I assumed that she was asleep with her ringer off. Unperturbed, I dressed Asia then got myself dressed. I stood in the full length mirror in my bedroom and combed my hair into a cute bun, pulled on some 7 for All Mankind faded jeans and a cute white baby tee with Boss Chick written in bold letters. I wanted to be a fly bitch when I fell up in visitation and told Prince face to face that I was moving on just as he had. I wished I could've taken Shaheed with me. Let Prince see that I was so not pressed.

When I was done putting the finishing touches on my makeup, I rolled Asia out to the car in her child sized wheelchair and helped her into the backseat. Fifteen minutes later we arrived at Mama's house on Edgewood.

Leaving Asia in the car, I went to the door and knocked. I got no answer, but she had to be inside because her car was in the driveway.

I knocked again, louder this time, but still no answer. Sighing, I reached in my Gucci bag and got the door key that I still kept from when I used to live at home.

"Mama," I called out as I stepped inside and looked around. Still no answer, and no sign of her. The tune of Teddy Pendergrass was playing from her bedroom in the back.

"What the fuck!" I bellowed and briskly walked to the back.

Mama's bedroom door was closed. I pressed my ear to the door just as the song ended.

"Lick it," I clearly heard my mother say. "Lick it slow, baby."

Oh no! no! no! I burst inside the bedroom shouting, "Mama! You ought to be ashamed of yourself!"

She shot up in bed with her hair and eyes looking wild. Mr. Sam was wearing no shirt. He had gray taco meat on his chest, and he wore black and white polka dot boxers. His silk socks were pulled up to his knees.

"You old fucker!" I cussed him. I ran toward him swinging, but Mama hopped up and pushed me back, butt naked. The whole scene made me sick on the stomach.

"Get out!" she ordered, standing there with a big hairy bush covering her stuff. It was awful!

I turned my back to them. "Where is his car?" I demanded to know like I was her mother instead of her being mine.

"It's in the garage," Mama shamelessly admitted as if the shit was cute or something.

I shook my head and left out, dialing Angie as I did. "Gurrl, you not gon' believe this!" I said as soon as she answered her phone.

By the time I finished telling her the story in vivid and disgusting detail, I was halfway back to my house. My sister was cracking the fuck up. I would've thought she would be furious with Mama, but she wasn't.

"Well, Mom has to get hers too." She burst out laughing.

"I understand that, Angie, but with Mr. Sam? That man is at least seventy years old. Mama ain't but fifty-one. I know she's not *that* desperate."

"Oh, Solange, get over it." She blew the whole incident off, but I couldn't get the image out of my head.

I was unable to visit Prince that day. It was as if something came up every time I planned to go see him. I did write him a letter though; telling him that I didn't appreciate him sending his bitch to my house to check on me.

Closing the letter, I softened a bit.

I'm no longer mad at you about it though. And please don't hold it against me that our baby was hit by a car. I am already feeling guilty enough. Be happy for me that I've found somebody that truly

132

loves me. I know that I haven't done right by you, and I apologize. I wasn't going to admit this, but I've had a change of heart so here it goes: I still have money of yours. I'm gonna put it up where you told me. If you ever get out it will be there. I hope this makes amends. Take care and I'll pray for your release.

Love,
Solange

A tear dripped from the corner of my eye as I sealed the envelope. I knew that part of my life was over. What I did not know at the time, was that I would never see Prince again.

Ca$h

Chapter 32
Prince

"**M**ail call!" the CO belted out.

Niggas crowded around hoping to hear their name called. I was leaned on the rail of the upper tier choppin' it up with Stack and Jabbo. Neither of us received mail frequently, so we weren't really listening to the names being called. It had been six months since I'd heard from Solange. I wasn't hot with her anymore because in her last letter she had come clean with me about everything. I'd tried to call her back then and thank her for being woman enough to tell the truth— which convinced me that she was at least trying to change— but her cell phone number had been changed. Through Mr. Sam, I kept up with how Asia was doing. She had fully recovered from her injuries, so I was good.

It was also a big relief that Solange hadn't fucked up all of my money. I didn't know exactly how much she had put up for me, because in her letters she hadn't said an amount, but anything beat nothing at all. Whenever I touched down, at least I wouldn't be broke. In the meantime, Nicole was holding me down as far as my needs on the inside were concerned, and she had taken care of the lawyers that were working on my appeal.

Just the other day I had spoken to my lead attorney on the phone. He had told me that a decision would be made soon, and from the vibe he got from his sources, things looked very favorable for reversal. I was cautiously excited.

"Prince Myers!" the C.O. called out, holding a letter above his head.

I walked down to the bottom tier to get my mail. I wondered who had written me. As soon as I saw 'Raven Campbell' as the sender, I knew the letter was from Nicole. We had not spoken on the phone in two days. I had to flush my cell phone down the toilet when the shakedown crew ran up in the block at two o'clock in the morning.

Nicole was gonna bring me another cell phone when she felt safe doing so. I tore open the letter and read her words as I walked to my cell and closed the door.

My Prince,

Baby, I'm missing you like crazy. I feel so lonely now that I can't hear your voice. My Love, I can't wait 'til there's a decision on your appeal. Every fiber in my body tells me that you're coming home. I simply can't wait for the day— it is all I can think about.

Baby, I dreamed that you were home. You were right here in the bedroom, making sweet love to me. You held me in your arms and kissed my shoulders as you glided in and out of me so deep and gentle. One day soon that will become reality. I love you so much. Don't worry, I'll have you back on deck soon.

Love,

Your Thug Princess

Damn, shawdy had a nigga bricked up. But more than her sensual nature, I was sprung on her devotion to me. I couldn't think of a single nigga at the prison whose girl rode harder than mine. Nicole was smooth with her shit, in spite of having all eyes on her at work. She was by far the baddest chick there. We managed to carry on without raising suspicion.

With Nicole holding me down, and my appeal looking good, shit was sweet. Little did I know, but things were about to take an unexpected turn for the worse.

Chapter 33
Solange

Asia was running around the house showing no signs of her injuries months ago. I was in the kitchen cooking tilapia, rice, and steamed vegetables. Shaheed walked in the living room with his cell phone pressed to his ear. "Bruh, that shit you sold me was some straight bullshit! Niggas complaining about it. You need to come get the rest of this wack ass shit. Matter of fact, bring me my dough before it gets serious!" I heard him say.

The creases in his forehead told me that he was a mile beyond mad. "Nigga must take me for a lame," he growled as he sat his cell down on the glass and brass end table.

"What is it, baby?" I asked from in the front of the range top stove.

"That nigga, Renegade, gon' make me get at him."

"Baby, I thought you wasn't dealing with him no more."

"I haven't been, but my connect ain't on deck right now. I had to fuck with this nigga, and now he done put me in the remix." He clearly was steaming.

"Humph," I replied, bringing him his plate. "Asia, are you ready to eat, baby?" I called out to my daughter.

"No, Mommie, can I eat later?" she called back from her bedroom. I considered it for a minute then decided that it would be okay. Tonight was Saturday and it was only eight o'clock.

"Yes, sweetie, you can eat later," I yelled back.

"Thanks, Mom."

Returning my attention to Shaheed, I sat down across from him at the kitchen table placing my plate in front of me. "Baby, eat your dinner," I said after noticing that he hadn't touched it.

"And you know what else, shawdy?" he asked me and cocked his head sideways before looking at me.

"What, boo?"

"That nigga confronted me on some bitch shit. Talkin' 'bout Tash told him that she heard that you been going around telling muthafuckas that we bodied Jamal."

"What!" I dropped my fork.

"That bitch just tryna start some shit," he pointed out. "Cause I know you know better than to do that."

"I sho' do! I'm gon' kick that ass. I have had enough of her shit. If she was a real bitch, she wouldn't have to put lies out there. She would step to me like a woman and straighten her business if she's still upset over that beat down I gave her," I snapped. Now, *my* appetite was gone.

"It's gucci, baby doll," said Shaheed letting out a long sigh, "Let's eat, fuck that messy ho." He picked his fork up and started smashing his food.

"I'ma fuck her alright. *Fuck her up!*"

My baby laughed then we both ate our dinner while discussing the new house we had decided to purchase. It was a four-bedroom ranch style out in Riversdale. I was so looking forward to moving. I had enrolled in Cosmetology School. Angie had convinced me to go ahead and better myself. Fuck partying. I hadn't been to the club since before Asia's accident. I hadn't planned to go back either.

I was complaining to Shaheed that going back to school after all those years was gonna really be difficult for me. "I may not be ready."

Boom!

All of a sudden, the back door came crashing in. "Ahhh!" I screamed.

Shaheed shot up from the table, probably tryna go after his strap in the bedroom.

Bop! Bop! Two shots dropped him face down.

"Never threaten a killa!" growled Renegade who had two other niggas with him. They all had guns and were masked. I knew it was

Renegade by his voice plus the fact that he and Shaheed had just had some words.

Shaheed was hit in the back. Blood oozed out of his chest and smeared the kitchen tile beneath him. Renegade stood over him sneering. "Nigga, fuck you think you was talking to? I ain't nothing nice." He aimed the gun down at Shaheed's skull and let off three rounds. Boc! Boc! Boc!

I screamed and covered my eyes with both hands. I did not want to remember Shaheed with his brains shot out.

"Shut up, bitch!" barked one of the two strangers. He slapped me in the mouth with his gun, dislodging several of my front teeth. My mouth filled with so much blood I coughed out globs of it.

Renegade came over and grabbed me by the hair, shoving his strap in my face. "Yeah, ho, I'm all up in this bitch now! You see what I did to yo' nigga. Look at him." He reached over and yanked my head toward Shaheed who was lying on the floor, lifeless.

"If you don't wanna end up beside him, you better take me to his stash." His two accomplices stood behind him with guns in their hands, staring me down.

"Okay," I whispered. "Please don't hurt me."

Just then my worst fear happened. Asia came running into the kitchen. "Mommie, what was that noise?" she asked me and paused once she noticed that strangers were in the house.

Renegade showed no mercy. "Snatch that lil' bitch up too," he bossed his boys.

"Not my baby!" I cried as body trembled with fear.

Oh, my God! If only Prince was here.

Ca$h

Chapter 34
Prince

"**U**nc, it's over wit, woady!" I walked into Jabbo's cell and announced with a wide smile that spread from one ear to the other.

"What you talkin' 'bout?" he asked as he slowly rose from his bottom bunk.

"They reversed my conviction. I just got off the phone with my lawyer and he gave me the news."

"That's a blessing." He cracked a short smile and looked off. Not out of jealousy, but I knew that he had grown to love me as a son and would miss me. He held his head back and nodded a few times like he was trying to let what I had just said sink in.

"Indeed it is. Man, they gonna let me out on an appeal bond tomorrow morning. The state will have thirty days to appeal the reversal, but my lawyers said it's useless because once the Supreme Court reverses a conviction they won't go back on it."

"That's good news, but will the state re-try you on the original charge?"

"It don't even matter, woady. Once I touch down they'll have to kill me before I come back to this muthafucka," I stated with conviction, and I wasn't frontin'. Nothing would send me back to prison.

Me and Jabbo went to share the news with Stack. He too was happy to see me win my appeal, but the moment was bittersweet. I realized that even in their happiness for me, they had to be wishing that it was them going home.

Later that night, I hit Nicole up on this other nigga's jack. She had made me sell the latest one that she brought me. *"I don't want anything to hold up your release,"* she made loud and clear, in anticipation of the court's decision.

When I hit her up, the first thing she did was scream with joy. She was already aware of the reversal. "I've already posted your bond. I'll be at the prison bright and early in the morning to pick you up."

"Baby, ain't that gonna compromise your job?" I asked with concern.

"No. I've already resigned," she informed me with a cheerful tone.

"A'ight, baby girl. I'll see you in the morning."

"Yes you will. See you in the morning, my love." She blew me a kiss and we said our goodbyes.

A nigga couldn't sleep a wink with freedom just hours away. I laid on my bunk all night mentally planning all the things I would do tomorrow. Every thought included getting out. Man, was Solange gonna be surprised when I pulled up there to get Asia!

I already knew that niggas who had left me for dead was gonna be acting like it was love. But, I didn't have no rap for any of them. All I needed was Nicole.

Morning came at a snail's pace. The hours ticked by excruciatingly slow. But finally around 7 a.m. Captain Lewis came to take me down to "discharge." That Uncle Tom nigga's face was twisted. He would have rather seen me with dick up his wife than going home. Then, when he saw who was there to pick me up, they had to call a medical emergency.

I was laughing as I hugged Nicole. I walked up out of there, hugging my boo. We stopped and looked back one last time at the captain receiving oxygen from the nurses. "Try not to hate," I yelled over my shoulder.

Chapter 35
Nicole

I stood there in the entrance of my door ready to do some things to Prince as I waited for him to come inside. He got out of my Benz parked inside the garage and placed his arms around my waist. After we hugged for a good two minutes straight, he slightly pushed me backwards and was checking me out from top to bottom. The hip hugging jeans and fuchsia tank top that I had on were ready to come off.

He smiled and pulled me into his arms and I led him to the master bedroom. "Damn, hot girl, you smelling all good and shit." He sniffed at my neck as we were walking.

"You lookin' good too, baby."

Admiring everything about the room, Prince said, "Yo' crib is bangin'. This shit is real nice."

"I'm glad that you like it," I said, thanking him for the compliment. "While you're taking a shower," I said, before I paused and pointed to the left at the huge bathroom. "I can fix you some breakfast because you're going to need a lot of energy for all of this." I slid my hand down my thigh and winked.

"Man, I can eat later. Right now I want you." He started tugging at my clothes.

"Let's take a shower together," I suggested and kissed him on his jaw.

"C'mon."

When I saw my baby's body hit that water, I was immediately aroused. He grabbed me into his arms and pulled my body into his. We started sharing a passionate kiss and rubbing all over each other. I reached between his legs and started to stroke him. His lips found their way to my neck, and I must admit that he was driving me insane.

"Baby, pick me up," I told him and closed my eyes enjoying his wet kisses that he had started placing under my chin.

He picked me up, and I wrapped my legs around his waist. He put my back against the shower wall and slid right inside of me.

"Ooooh, yessss," I said as soon as I felt him push himself deeper. He was moving in and out of me making my body feel so good. "Prince, go deeper!" I demanded with my arms wrapped around his neck and shoulder. He grabbed me around my waist with a tight grip and brought my body down on his with force.

"I love you, baby," I purred into his ear.

"I love you, too." He pushed in me harder. No words could describe the way he was making me feel. He had my mind all messed up with the way he was giving it to me. And after he pounded my kitty real good and deep for what seemed like forever, I was ready to come all over him.

I let out, "Oh, baby, I'm about to come." I spilled my fluids all over his erection. Soon after Prince was filling me up with his. I held on to him and regained my composure. We showered together with the warm water streaming down on us.

After washing each other's bodies, rinsing off, and then toweling each other dry, we returned to my bedroom. The two of us climbed in my king sized bed and talked about our hopes and dreams and the life we planned on building together. He had put it on me so good that while he was talking, I drifted off to sleep in his arms.

I didn't have a single worry in the world. My Prince was home. Not even his petty baby mama could ruin this moment.

Chapter 36
Solange

"**I** swear that's all the money Shaheed had here," I cried and begged Renegade to believe me. I was on my knees looking up to him from my bedroom floor where he had pushed me down.

He looked inside the shoe bag that I knew contained $70,000. His face was contorted into something very frightening. "Bitch!" he spat. "That nigga had way more dough than this— you wanna play games?"

"No, I swear, that's all he kept here." It was the God honest truth, but Renegade didn't believe me.

"Dog, check up under the bed. I know her and how she get down, she's three quarters slick," he said to the taller of his two partners who was heavy set.

The guy searched under the bed but came out empty-handed. There was nothing to be found, and this made Renegade furious. He drew back and punched me in the eye, almost knocking it out of socket. "Leave my mommy alone," Asia bravely cried out.

"Tone, take that lil' bitch out of here before I do something real foul to her," he barked.

By now, the eye he punched me in was closed. Out of the other eye, I saw the other dude drag Asia out by her arm. "Please don't hurt my baby," I pleaded.

"Well, you better act right," Renegade said unzipping himself.

My mouth was swollen and caked with dried blood, but Renegade didn't care. He forced himself in my mouth and pumped in and out. The strong smell of piss and musty balls caused me to throw up all over the place. I gagged on blood and vomit.

Like a twisted maniac Renegade seemed to be enjoying my humiliation. "Now clean me up, bitch!" he spat, tossing me the blanket off the bed.

I did as he asked. I was praying that my compliance would spare me and my child's lives. After I had wiped the vomit off of him as best I could, he demanded to know where Shaheed kept his money. I considered claiming not to know, but I shuddered at the thought of the consequences that reply would have brought. So I said, "He keeps it at his mom's house on Cascade Road."

He thought for a minute, and then he grabbed my cell phone off the nightstand, with his gloved hand, and made me call Shaheed's mother. The problem was, Shaheed's mom would not go for any lies I concocted to get her to give up his money. Finally, she just hung up on me.

"I tried," I said looking up at Renegade with fear in my eyes for failing to accomplish what he had ordered me to do. I begged him not to blow my brains out.

"We going to the bitch's house. Where does she live?" He was becoming irate. I had only been to Shaheed's mother's house once, but I was damn sure gonna do my best to recall where she lived. I would do anything to save me and Asia's lives. I was desperate.

A gun was kept to my head as I rode in the backseat between Renegade's mans' out to Cascade Road. Asia was strapped in the front passenger seat, and Renegade was behind the wheel of the dark colored Suburban we rode in. The sky was as dark as my thoughts. I kept seeing images of Shaheed leaking blood from his head onto my kitchen floor. I wondered why God had chosen this fate for me after I had finally changed my life.

Things quickly worsened when I could not remember where Shaheed's mother lived. Renegade pounded his fist against the steering wheel out of anger.

He turned onto a dark road, parked, and they dragged me and my poor little baby out the truck slingin' us both to the ground.

"Get right with God, bitch, because you're headed to meet him," Renegade barked down at me. Before I could plead for mercy, I saw gun sparks. Then I felt a burn shoot through my side.

146

Bap! Bap! He mercilessly shot me twice more. Blood quickly filled up the holes he shot inside of my body. *Lord, please don't let him kill my baby,* I prayed.

God heard my prayer. Renegade and his heartless friends hopped back in the truck without harming Asia. They drove off, tires spinning.

I laid on the cold concrete, dying, with my baby in my arms. She was crying, "Mommie, don't die."

I struggled to speak because I was choking on my own blood. Somehow I managed to gurgle, "Go get help." I pointed toward a light far in the distance.

"Okay, Mommie," Asia bravely replied and removed herself from my arms.

"I—love—you—" I pushed out.

I held on to life until my baby was up the road. Then I closed my eyes and went home with Jesus.

Ca$h

Chapter 37
Prince

A nigga was in heaven. Freedom was the sweetest thing a nigga could ever have. And mine was enhanced by the beautiful woman lying in my arms.

"Girl, you're a beast." Nicole had really put it down. Making love to her for the first time without having to hurry or to worry about getting caught was indescribable. I had bust off fast the first time, but once she sucked me back hard I had shown her that I was not a Minute Man.

"Mmmm'," she moaned. It was all she could do because I had taken her down through there, around there, and back again. Now that ass was knocked out.

"See, that's what that thug dick do to you," I teased rubbing up and down her shoulder.

"Hush, fool," she said, giggling with her head on my chest.

"Damn, baby. I need a blunt," I sighed.

"You won't find one here. A glass of OJ will have to do," she replied rubbing my chest.

"Stop wit' the jokes." I chuckled.

"I'm sorry, babe."

"It's all good. I'ma just lay here and hold my girl in my arms."

"Mmm."

Nicole dozed back off. I held her until she awoke a half hour later, and then I greeted her with a kiss.

Later, after we had showered together and made love under the water spray, I dressed in the Dolce & Gabbana t-shirt and denim jeans that she had bought me. I sat on the edge of the bed delightfully watchin' her get dressed. She was pulling up her denim Armani skinny jeans and already had on a black baby tee with Armani embroidered across the front. We were about to head to Atlanta, so that

149

I could see Asia. I hadn't seen my baby in almost a year. I couldn't wait to see the smile on her face when she saw me.

"Maybe, you should call Mr. Sam and ask him if Solange and Asia are at home," Nicole suggested. "If they are, just ask him not to tell them that you're out." She laughed and further said, "Cause you know he has a big mouth."

I nodded in agreement, sat up in the bed and held my hand out. "Yeah, I'ma do that. Let me use your phone."

When I called Mr. Sam, I got the shock of my life. "What do you mean they found Solange's boyfriend's dead body inside the house and she and Asia are missing?" I repeated his words back to him in the form of a question to make sure I had heard him correctly.

"I'm sorry, Prince, but it's true. They say it was a lot of blood in that house, but I'm praying that the police will find Solange and your daughter somewhere safe and sound," he said, sounding very upset and sad at the same time.

"Aight, man. I'm on my way up there. I just got out this morning and now this!" I steamed. I got off the phone with Mr. Sam then I called Solange's mother.

Her mom was too hysterical for me to understand what she was saying, so Angie came on the line. I had never gotten along with her because she was a real bougie bitch that had her nose turned. She was some sort of distinguished professional. Considering the circumstances, she sounded glad that I was out, though we both were worried about Solange and Asia.

"Where could they be?" she cried.

I told her that I had no idea but, I was coming up there to get some answers.

"And if I don't like the answers I get, it's gon' be the bloodiest summer Atlanta has ever seen," I vowed.

When I got off the phone Nicole was staring at me. She had pieced together what was going on from my end of the conversation, and I filled in the rest. "Oh my God!" she fretted.

"I need to use your car," I told her while I called my nigga Cap to make arrangements to get my hands on a banger once I touched down in the city.

My nigga said it wouldn't be a problem, he had straps on deck. "How did you get out?" he asked.

"They overturned my conviction." I kept it brief. He had heard on the news what happened at Solange's house.

"Shawdy, you ain't have nothing to do with that shit, did you?"

"Hell no, bruh. You know my daughter is my life. I'm about to come up there and turn the city inside out lookin' for mine. And may God help the whole city if my shortie ain't alive when I find her."

Nicole's pleas for me to let the police handle it fell on deaf ears. I understood her concerns— she had risked everything to help win my freedom, and now I was about to endanger it again—but when it came to Asia, fuck freedom and everything else.

I had to literally *take* Nicole's car keys from her. We tussled all over the bedroom until she finally let go of the key ring and flopped down on the bed in tears.

I sat down beside her, wrapped an arm around her shoulders, and tried to explain. "Baby, I'm not gonna do nothin' foolish. I'ma go up there and hit the streets to try to find my daughter. I realize all that you sacrificed for me to be here with you, and I'm not just gonna throw it away. But this is something that neither of us could have predicted. Trust me to handle this and come back to you, ok?" I lifted her chin and looked in her eyes.

"Okay, baby." She gave me her blessings which ended the tug-of-war that had been going on inside of me.

It took three hours for me to get to Atlanta from Claxton, Georgia where Nicole lived. I tried to remain optimistic about Solange's and Asia's well-being as I did ninety miles per hour all the way there. I believed that the two years that I had spent in prison, almost hopeless until Nicole came into my life, had changed me for the better. Hustlin' was no longer on my mind, but the beast within was still present. I knew that I would not even resist its roar to take shit to the streets if my seed had been harmed.

In the streets, violence was dealt with more violence. That was the code that I learned growing up in Nawlins, and that was what I had lived by. I pulled up at my niggas crib on Atlanta's Westside to get the banger he had promised me. I thought about the consequences of taking the law into my own hands. If I bodied someone and got caught I would end up like Jabbo and 'em, locked up with no hope of ever gettin' out.

But my little girl was worth my life. Straight the fuck up!

My nigga, Cap, was happy to see me back onthe bricks. We G-hugged and chopped it up briefly, and then he gave me a fo-fifth and an extra clip. I tucked it in my waist and bounced, saying, "I'll be in touch, family."

I left there and drove straight over to Solange's house. Yellow and black crime scene tape crisscrossed across the front door. I shook my head. I was gonna go ham if Asia wasn't safe.

Mr. Sam couldn't tell me anything more than he had already told me. So I left there and went over to Solange's mother, Miss Shirley's house.

When I arrived there Miss Shirley and Angie were both a mess. They feared that the outcome was not gonna be good. Miss Shirley was babbling spiritual prayers, rocking back and forth on the living room sofa. She seemed to have aged terribly since I had seen her three years ago. I knew it was the stress of not knowing if Solange and Asia was okay. Angie, whom I had never seen less than lady-like and proper, was pacing back and forth wringing her hands. Other family members, cousins, aunts, and so forth, crowded the house. Everyone was worried, but no one was doing a goddamn thing to find them. Not even the police, it seemed.

"What was the dude's name Solange was dealing with?" I questioned Angie. Fuck sitting around looking sad. I was about to go on a hunt.

"Shaheed," she said. That was a start.

I hit the block and found that this dude Shaheed had a partna named Renegade. Several people told me that Renegade fucked with a bitch named Tash who I knew well. That ho was Solange's best friend.

Before I could locate Tash I received a call from Angie. I knew that the news was bad the minute I said "hello" and she broke down sobbing. "Angie, tell me something," I shouted.

"They found Solange and Asia's bodies," she wept.

I dropped the cell phone on the floorboard, pulled over to the side of the road, leaned my head against the steering wheel and cried for my seed. I cried long and hard. Nothin' in my lifetime had ever hurt worse.

Ca$h

Chapter 38
Nicole

My heart sunk when Prince called and told me the sad news. The pain in his voice transmitted through the phone and I could tell that he was hurting bad. I asked, "Where are you, baby? Let me come to you."

"Na, shawdy, stay where you're at. I'm about to turn all the way up."

"Prince, what does that mean?" I feared the answer.

"Watch the news and count the bodies, but don't count on your fingers and toes because you ain't got enough of them." The line went dead.

I called back again and again, but I was repeatedly sent to voicemail. I slammed my house phone down on the floor in emotions of anger, frustration, hurt, and worry. I wanted to curl up in a ball and cry. The more I thought about what Prince was feeling and what someone had done to Solange and his daughter, the less angry I was about what I knew he was about to do.

I called Raven and asked if she would come over. I really needed my bestie to talk some sense into me because I was seriously contemplating going up to Atlanta and being Bonnie to Prince's Clyde.

"An eye for an eye...so sayeth The Lord." I tried to defend my thinking to Raven as we discussed it sitting at my kitchen table over two cups of steaming coffee.

"Oh Lord, Nicole, you are not thinking sensibly. Let's just hope that the police arrest whoever did it, before Prince finds them. In the meantime, I am not letting you leave this house." Raven appealed to my better judgment.

So all I could do was sit at home and worry about Prince because he still would not answer the phone.

Ca$h

Chapter 39
Prince

We stood at the scene when the bodies had been found. Miss Shirley and Angie embraced each other while the coroner unzipped the larger body bag so that Solange could be identified.

Miss Shirley braved a peek, and then she fell to the ground sobbing and pounding her hand against the hard soil. "Why Lord... why?" she cried.

Angie was down on her knees trying fruitlessly to console her mother. It was left to me to identify Asia's body. When the coroner unzipped that small body bag, and I saw dried blood all over my baby, and her face contorted in fear, even in death— I closed my eyes and shuddered in rage. What type of soulless muthafucka would do that to a child? I asked myself as a tear escaped my eye.

Muthafuckas were gonna pay. That wasn't a threat; that was a promise.

Two nights later, I creeped up behind Tash just as she was climbing into her Nissan Maxima. I pressed my strap against the back of her head and shoved her down on the floor of the car. "Bitch, I want some answers!" I growled.

"About what?" she cried.

I snatched her head up by the back of her weave and twisted it so that she could see my face. "Prince!" she gasped out of fear. Her eyes were jumping and her hands were trembling.

"Yeah, bitch, it's me. You got five seconds to tell me what Renegade had to do with Solange and Asia being killed. Five—four— three—two..." My trigger finger was ready to squeeze in another second.

"Wait! I'll tell you everything, just don't kill me," she begged.

"Talk!" I barked and clocked her upside the head with the butt of my heater.

After she let out a long moan from me rapping that head with my steel, I listened as she told me that her nigga and two of his boys were responsible for what had happened. "They weren't supposed to kill Solange and Asia. Me and Solange may have fallen out with each other, but I still loved her and Asia was my god-daughter. I swear on my mother's grave that I had nothing to do with it. You have to believe…"

Boc! Boc!

Her head exploded all over the front seat.

"I don't have to believe shit, bitch," I said to her corpse that jumped a few times before it completely stopped moving.

Chapter 40
Nicole

I hadn't heard from Prince since the day the bodies of Solange and Asia was discovered and here it was the day of the funerals. Raven accompanied me as I entered the holy doors of Mount Cornnel Baptist Church in Atlanta where the services were being held.

I wore an all-black ruffle blouse, a black pencil skirt by Nicole Miller, and black open toe Jimmy Choo heels. My hair hung down my back in a wrap. Black shades covered my red eyes as they searched the pews for Prince. I didn't see him anywhere inside the church.

Raven guided me to vacant seats near the back of the pews. The church was packed from wall to wall; the grief was so heavy inside there that it made my heart ache. The organist played, *'Oh Precious Lord'* as everyone stood in respect for the family when they entered the church. Still no Prince.

The minister was thirty minutes into his sermon when Prince walked in, head down, and shoulders slumped. He looked up and saw me. "Thanks for coming," he said right above a whisper before joining Solange's family in the front row.

I suppose it was selfish of me to feel some kind of way about that, but it is how I felt. Probably because we hadn't talked in a week, and I felt blocked out of his life. I wanted to be there at this time of tragedy. The sad expression on his face confirmed that he was crushed inside.

Reading my thoughts, Raven put a hand on top of mine. "He's hurting," she leaned over and whispered in my ear. "And you're hurting for him. Just give it time and it will all work out."

I needed to hear those words.

The minister's sermon jerked tears from every set of eyes in the church, including mine. I was so relieved when he ended the sermon.

I could not have taken another sad word. Now it was time to view the bodies. "I can't do it," I whispered to Raven.

"He'll understand, if he notices," she whispered back.

I glanced up and saw Prince and the family somberly approaching the caskets. My heart ached for the one I loved.

Chapter 41
Prince

Grief weighed on me heavier than anything that I had ever had to face. It was much heavier than the troubles I had felt when I was serving life behind the bricks before my appeal was won. My little dimple-smiled angel was gone; murdered with no compassion for her innocence.

I stood up in a catatonic state of mind. I walked up to the stage where Asia's and Solange's bodies were laid out for viewing. They were in identical light pink caskets with flower arrangements around them. My footsteps were slow with all the hurt and pain that I felt inside. I felt a strong amount of guilt because, had I never gone to prison none of this would have happened.

In front of me Miss Shirley, Angie, and Mr. Sam were the first to view the bodies. Miss Shirley fainted into Mr. Sam's arms after briefly looking down into the caskets. The funeral director rushed up and assisted Mr. Sam with helping her back to her seat. Angie burst out in tears so loud that a chorus of sobs joined with hers.

I swallowed hard when it was my turn to step up to the caskets. I wasn't ready to look down at my daughter so I viewed Solange first. She was dressed in a soft pink dress with a high collar. Her hair was in loose curls with two bangs that hung down framing her face. She looked beautiful, but not at peace. Maybe it was just me, but it seemed that her expression begged me to find her killer. At the same time, I recalled our many battles after I was locked up. None of that mattered now.

I put my hand on her shoulder and said, "Rest in peace, baby mama."

Asia's casket was directly to the right of Solange's. It took all that a nigga had to step up to that casket and look down at my little girl with her eyes closed for eternity. Fathers weren't supposed to bury their daughters, but those ruthless muthafuckas that had done this to her was gonna get dealt with; without remorse when I caught up with 'em.

Daddy's sorry, my angel, I thought as I looked down into Asia's innocent face. She was dressed in a white dress edged with white and pink ruffles, and a princess crown sat beautifully on her head. I leaned over and placed a kiss on her lips. "You're in God's arms now, baby girl. Nothing and no one can ever hurt you again."

No tears fell from my eyes. I had shed so many the past few days. Now the tears were replaced with anger. Renegade and 'em were gonna suffer for what they did to mine!

A soft hand touched my arm. I looked up to see Nicole at my side. I took her hand in mine as we stood there another minute with Asia.

At Pleasant Hills cemetery, Asia and Solange were laid to rest side by side. The gravesite sermon from the minister evoked more tears from Miss Shirley, Angie and other mourners present. I said a final goodbye to my daughter and her mother, and then I gave Nicole her car keys. "Go back home. If I never make it back to you, you know that I loved you," I told her as she, Raven, and I proceeded to their cars.

"Prince," Nicole started to protest but I shut her down.

"Nicole, nothin'—and I mean nothin' can stop me," I stated emphatically.

"Please be careful," she said. She must have realized that I was gonna do what I had to do.

"I will," I promised, and then I slid into my nigga Cap's whip. He had been waiting at the curb. I'd called him on my way to the cemetery.

"Sup, woady," I greeted him. "I hope you're ready to put in work 'cause I'm about to set the city on fiyah lookin' for those niggas."

Cap nodded his head. It was do-or-die from here on out.

In Love With a Convict

Chapter 42
Prince

Renegade was well known in the city and he was also disliked by many because he sold bad product and wasn't adverse to puttin' niggas in the remix. Another thing that worked against him was that he had shitted on several females who were thirsty to see him get what he deserved. Then too, the streets talk, so niggas had heard that he was responsible for Solange and Asia's murders. Nobody would protect a heartless baby killer.

Cap drove me to the stash spot where Solange had told me in her last letter that she had put my dough. I found it exactly where it was supposed to be. It was a little more than ninety bands. I gave Cap twenty, as I had promised for him to ride on Renegade and 'em with me. Then I played the background while he dropped money to different niggas for info on those we were looking for.

We found out that the two niggas that more than likely had been Renegades accomplice was named Tone and Bear, and that they slung yams outta a room on Fulton Industrial.

We waited until dark fell and went to serve them street justice. When we pulled into the parking lot of the business across from the motel where Tone and Bear was said to be, we saw the flashing lights of police cruisers in the motel's lot.

I put my banger under the seat and slid out of the whip. I walked across the street and blended in with the crowd that had formed outside the motel. "What happened?" I asked a lady with old school pink cushion rollers in her hair.

"They just arrested those two boys that be selling drugs outta room 212. They saying they're the ones who killed that girl and her baby— the ones that's been on the news lately," she informed me.

"Damn," I thought, why did po po have to find those niggas before I did? Just then, detectives led two dudes out of room 212 in handcuffs, down to awaiting unmarked cars. One of the dudes wore a full Rick Ross beard, the other wore dreads. I stared fire at those bitch ass niggas. Fate had robbed me of my revenge. Now I had to locate Renegade fast.

Finding Renegade wasn't as easy for me as it was for the police. That nigga had gotten ghost.

As early spring passed by, his mans remained in custody charged with double homicide. They were facing the death penalty for the callous murder of Solange and Asia. The AJC reported both of those niggas sang like some birds. They described to police the murder of Shaheed, then the kidnapping of Solange and Asia.

According to their statements, alleged fugitive Ken Jones, alias Renegade became furious after the deceased Solange Micheals could not remember where Shaheed Parks' mother lived. He drove Solange and her child to a place where their bodies were found, and the three men drug the mother and child out of the vehicle. Allegedly, Ken Jones executed the mother, and then the three men got back inside the vehicle and drove off, leaving little Asia unharmed. It is then alleged that Ken Jones decided that he was going back and kill the child. According to both suspects in custody, Asia was spotted running in the dark road crying for help.

In closing, the article quoted Tony "Tone" Edwards final words in his written statement to police. It read, *Going back to where he had left Solange and the little girl running up that dark street. Renegade stopped the car and hopped out. Asia tried to run faster but he ran her down. He dragged her back to the car then drove her back to where he had left her mother's body. I begged him not to hurt the little girl, but he put the gun to my head and told me to shut up. I couldn't even look when he dragged that baby out the car. I knew he was gonna kill her. All I heard were the shots. I heard Boc! Boc! Then he came back to the car and said, "No witnesses!"*

I let the article fall to the floor and my hands shook with fury like a volcano threatening to erupt. My baby's last moments had to have been terrifying. *Renegade gonna suffer like the dog he is*, I vowed to myself.

Ca$h

Chapter 43
Nicole

A full week passed after the funerals. I had been back in Claxton biting my nails down to the meat of my fingers every day that Prince remained in Atlanta intent on seeking vengeance. I understood his pain. I just didn't want it to end with him in prison again.

"Baby, please be careful. I won't be able to go on if something happens to you. Already, I can't eat or sleep. I promise you I've grown a gray hair or two since this happened," I had told him earlier in the day when he called.

"I'm good. Try not to worry. I promise to make it home to you." He'd tried to ease my worries, but his words helped little. I just didn't let him know that.

"Okay, baby. Are you eating?" I asked out of concern.

"Na. I ain't had no appetite."

"Hmm. That's not good, honey. Your body needs nourishment or else your mind isn't as sharp as it should be."

"I'm good, baby. Don't worry."

"I can't help it, Prince."

"I know." He understood.

"Baby, where are you staying?" I asked.

He gave me the name and the location of the motel on Old National Highway where he had a room. I jotted it down in my memory. "Prince, please be careful," I repeated for the one-millionth time.

"I got you," he reassured. "I'ma hit you up tomorrow, okay. Love you."

"Love you more," I said from the heart.

Sitting in the living room of my new place, an hour after hanging up from Prince, I was startled by the chime of the doorbell. My nerves were really bad. Figuring that it was Raven, I went to the door and opened it. Anthony stood there with a wrapped fruit basket with a big bow on the front. I guess the gift was for me. Hmph, I wasn't thinking about his ass.

"Did Amber die or something?" I sneered.

"No, Nicole. May I come in?" he asked.

"I don't think so!" My sarcasm was toxic.

"Please, Nicole, just for a minute. All I ask is that you hear me out."

I slammed the door in that bastard's face. "I can hear just fine like this," I said from the other side of the door with a smirk because I knew that I was hurting his feelings. He needed to hurt, the same way he had hurt mine. I couldn't stand the sight of him.

"Alright, Nicole, if this is how I must do it, then fine." He cleared his throat. "It turned out that Amber's baby isn't mine."

My mouth literally dropped, and I felt like joyously spinning around in circles. The fucker had held that tramp's pregnancy over me like a trophy. Now he was feeling like a clown at the circus. Dumb ass! That was good for him.

"Well, sounds like you'll be a step-dad." I burst out laughing.

"Nicole, that wasn't a very nice thing to say. What has gotten into you? I came here to apologize and ask if we can try it again," he had the balls to say. I swear, I was thinking that he had to forget to pay his brain bill because that was the dumbest thing he could have fixed his mouth to say to me.

I almost died laughing.

"What's so funny? Are you ridiculing me? Am I not thugged out enough for you? I heard about your little felon," he announced in an pompous manner.

"Have you?" I returned his question with a question. Before he could blurt out his answer, I went on. "Because my little felon, as you refer to him, is everything that you weren't and will never be. And I'm not just talking about in the bed," I purposely slung in his face. I hoped that last comment would deflate is huge ego. In my opinion, his ego was a whole lot larger than his little penis. And who the hell was he to stand there and talk down on Prince? My boo may have been a felon, but he was much more man than Anthony.

"Nicole, you're going to regret this. When you end up in prison along with your little thug, don't bother to call me to rescue you," he said.

Ha! I wouldn't ask him to spit on me if I was on fire. I snatched open the door and smiled at him sarcastically. "As my thug man might say, *Anthony, suck my dick!*" I grabbed the crotch of my pajamas like I really had a pole in my pants.

His face blushed and his mouth hung agape.

"Close your mouth, Anthony, before I stick my dick in it," I said. Then I slammed the door in his face once and for all. I doubled over in laughter at myself.

I started doing that dance called the Dougie. I sang, *"Teach me how to Dougie..."*

"Nicole, you are becoming thugged out." Raven laughed when I repeated the incident to her. But in the following days, my laughter evaporated like a drop of water in the desert.

Repeated calls to Prince were sent straight to voice mail. In a panic, I grabbed my car keys and headed back to Atlanta.

Ca$h

Chapter 44
Prince

My hunt for Renegade was coming up empty everywhere I searched. In my frustration, I was becoming careless. I had asked too many muthafuckas about him and where he might have been hiding out. I had told several dudes where I was laying my head in case they needed to get at me when they heard something. I had lost the cell phone that Nicole had copped for me and hadn't taken the time to buy another one yet. I was too busy on the prowl, in search of Renegade.

I couldn't recall my baby's second cell phone number. Therefore, I hadn't called her in three days. I knew that she'd be worried to death, but she would be alright. Shawdy was a whole different kind of strong.

Cap was still riding shotgun with a nigga, ready to put in work to earn that dough I had given him. It was Cap who found out that Renegade had a baby mama named Apryl. We had known that for weeks, but we had not been able to find out where the bitch lived.

One day we finally got a break.

Cap slid through and scooped me up from the room; he was hyped. "What it is, fool?" I asked as we pulled out into traffic.

"Nigga, I just found out that Renegade's baby mama, Apryl, works at a hair salon out on Covington Highway. It was so hard to find the ho because she don't fuck with that nigga no more," Cap went on to explain.

"If she don't fuck with him, how is it gon' help me to snatch her up? Also, if you found the bitch, you can bet the popo have too," I pointed out.

"Yeah, you right. Let's go check it out anyway. You never know." I shrugged and reached over and turned his radio on and listened to the Hip Hop station on the air.

That day we followed Apryl home from her job. For two days we watched her while watching for popos too. I found out that she had a daughter about Asia's age. A cute lil' chubby high yellow girl with so much energy. The girl skipped everywhere she went, no matter how short the distance. Watching the child made my heart ache even more for the one that I had lost. I wanted Renegade to feel my pain.

"Bruh, we snatchin' 'em up tonight," I told Cap on the third night of our stakeout. I was sure that no police were watching them. Being a street dude, I would've spotted those muthafuckas a mile away.

"I'm ready," Cap said, pulling out his banger as we rode toward Apryl's crib.

We waited until it was dark and the neighborhood was quiet, and then we kicked in the back door of the small house that sat near the end of the residential street. We were both dressed in all black and rocked ski masks over our faces.

The inside of Apryl's crib was like a statement that she believed in Jesus! There were different pictures of black Jesus decorating the walls of every room. As we searched the house, the sound of Shirley Caesar played in the background. I led Cap upstairs toward the sound of the music.

"Sssh." I twisted my neck in his direction and put my finger to my lips as we approached the bedroom where the music was coming from. With a gloved hand, I quietly twisted the doorknob and eased the door open. My fo-fifth was anxious to go off. I didn't know if that nigga, Renegade, was in there with her or not.

The lighting in Apryl's room was dim, but I could clearly see her kneeled in prayer at the side of her bed with her back facing me.

My eyes suddenly scanned the room for Renegade. I knew what the bitch nigga looked like from his mug shots on TV.

There was no sign of him being there.

"Check the other bedrooms," I whispered to Cap who was on my heels ready to let his nine milli spit some fire.

Cap headed in another direction leaving me to ease up behind Apryl and cover her mouth with one hand while the other pressed the banger to the back of her head.

Ca$h

Chapter 45
Nicole

I hadn't been able to take it a second longer. Not knowing if Prince was okay was driving me crazy. Stupid as it may sound, I hopped in my car and drove to Atlanta to rescue my man if he was in trouble. I was not going empty handed. Inside my Gucci bag was a can of mace and a stun gun. I had learned how to handle weapons during my years of training with the Bureau of Prisons.

Once in Atlanta, I used my GPS to find the motel on Old National Highway where he told me he was staying. *Room 114,* I repeated to myself as I pulled in front of the correct room and parked. The light above the doors illuminated the room numbers.

I knew that he would be furious with me for coming, but in my state of mind I did not care. I grabbed my bag off the passenger seat, got out of the car and locked the doors, and then turned on the alarm. Taking a deep breath before proceeding, I walked up to room 114 and knocked two times.

The door slightly opened and I stepped inside in a huff. "Boy, you had me so worried about you!" I went off. I squinted my eyes in the darkness of the room to see his reaction.

Whap! He slapped me to the floor! Then I felt a hand at my throat and the tip of the gun against my forehead. "Bitch, if you scream I'ma silence you forever," he threatened.

The voice did not belong to Prince. *Oh my God!*

***

Prince

Apryl shivered as I forced her to sit on the bed, and Cap brought her daughter into the room. "What do you want?" she cried with her face in her palms.

One word was all that I had to say. "Renegade."

"Are you the police? Of course not," she said on second thought.

"It don't matter who I am. Tell me where that nigga's at or I'm leave two bodies up in this bitch when I leave."

"I don't have any idea where Renegade is. I have not dealt with him in three years. I left him alone after I got saved and I'm glad that I did. A year later he contracted HIV. God is good." She waved her hand in the air like she was praising the Lord and thanking him for sparing her life.

"What?" I asked. I was shocked.

"Yes. The health department sent some papers to my house thinking he still lived here, I guess. I contacted him, and he had to be tested and so did I. He caught it six months after we broke up. After that, I turned my life over to Jesus. She paused for a minute. "I've seen on the news that he is wanted for killing a mother and her daughter. That is so awful if he did it. I'm just glad that he's no longer a part of me and Asiana's lives."

Huh? What did she just say? I asked myself. No, that couldn't be what she said. The bitch was running boss game.

"Woady, bring that little girl over here," I told Cap.

My nigga led the lil' shawdy over to where I stood over her mother. Her hands were shaking and her eyes were pleading for me not to hurt them. For a second I considered removing the ski mask so that I wouldn't look as frightening but that definitely would not have been smart. Instead I said, "You don't have to be afraid. Would you like to sit on the bed next to your Mommie?"

She didn't speak but she nodded, "yes."

"Okay go ahead and climb up there." She hopped up on the bed and Apryl hugged her to her chest. I allowed them to have a few seconds.

I asked the girl, "What's your name?"

"Asiana," she softly replied.

Damn, it couldn't have been a coincidence that her name was almost the same as Asia's. Was God trying to tell me something?

I believed everything that Apryl had said. It was good that she hadn't kept fucking with that grimey nigga. She could have had the same disease that he was walking around spreading like a wildfire. Why serve her some tragedy because of what Renegade did? She had turned her life around and left his sorry ass alone so I wouldn't punish her for his actions. Furthermore, there was no way I was killing a mother and a child after experiencing that same loss myself. My baby's name was Asia, shawdy's name was Asiana. That wasn't no coincidence.

Apryl looked at me. "Look, I'm not sure what this is about, but I don't deal with him on that level. The only thing that we share now is a daughter. After I turned my life over to God; I don't deal with men period. Until God sends the right one I'm remaining solo, but I just pray that God will touch your hearts and you'll have mercy on me and my baby and let us live."

I had no business up in that woman's house, threatening their lives. I said to Apryl, "Miss Lady, I'm not going to harm y'all, but let me ask you something. Do you have Renegade's number?"

"Yes," she admitted.

"Okay, I need you to call him. Can you do that?"

"I'm not sure that he'll answer, but I can try," she said.

I wasn't sure that Renegade would answer his phone either. The nigga was on the run for capital murders. His accomplices were already under arrest and blaming everything on him. The nigga was probably in the wind by now, I assumed. But you never knew; I had seen dudes do crazier shit and stick around.

Apryl stood and went over to the wall socket where her phone was plugged by the corner of the wall charging on the nightstand. She scrolled through her contacts. I was standing over her shoulder making sure that she didn't dial 911.

I saw her stop at the contact listed as Ken. Renegade's government name, which I knew from newspaper articles.

"Put the phone on speaker," I told Apryl as it began to ring.

I was praying he would answer, but on the real, I was surprised when he did.

"Yeah," said the muthafucka who had murdered my seed.

Chapter 46
Nicole

I so was terrified I could hardly breathe. Renegade stood over me, smirking. "Looking for Prince?" he jeered.

His face and voice were demonic. Knowing what he had done to Solange and little Asia made me even more afraid. I had to quickly think. "I don't know anyone by that name. I must have come to the wrong room looking for my husband. I'm..."

"Shut up, bitch! I hate liars. I saw you at the funeral holding hands with the nigga. Now I want you to call him up and get him to come here, but first I'm gonna fuck you real good and leave you with something to remember me by." Renegade chuckled. He unbuckled his pants and pulled his penis out.

I scooted away.

"Get back here, bitch. What, you scared of this big ass dick? It ain't gonna kill you. Oh, on second thought, it probably will," he said showing all of his teeth with that ugly smile of his. He roared with laughter that I couldn't understand. If it was some kind of joke, he had definitely lost me.

My back hit up against the foot of the chair, I could go no further. "Where are you tryna run to, girl? I got some good killa dick, and I love running it up you red hos. C'mere, open your mouth and suck it, and if you bite it I'm gon' puff your wig out," threatened the demon hovering over me.

I didn't know what to do, but I knew that I was not about to submit to being raped and sodomized. If either one of those things happened, it would be after he had killed me. I shook my head and said, "No. I am not doing that."

"Oh, bitch you gonna do it!"

Bop! He backhanded me.

My head hit the nightstand and I saw stars. *You should have stayed your behind in Claxton,* said the voice inside my head. But how could I be foolish for coming to see about the man I loved?

Renegade reached down and ripped open my blouse. "Please don't," I muttered as I scrambled away on my hands and knees.

"That's how I'm go up in you, just like that, doggystyle." He snickered sinisterly.

As I scurried across the floor in the dark, my head brushed up against a familiar object. It was my Gucci bag. I stopped in that spot telling myself not to panic.

The sound of a cell phone ringing seemed to stop Renegade in his tracks. *Answer it! Answer it!* I prayed.

To my surprise and relief, the maniac actually stopped to answer the phone! That proved to me that he was a cold killer, poised and not panicked.

"Hello?" I overheard him say. "Who is this? Apryl?"

I didn't know who the hell Apryl was, but hopefully she could keep his attention while I figured out what my next move would be.

Prince

"Na, nigga this ain't Apryl, and it ain't po po either. You know who this is. I got Apryl and Asiana over here trembling," I replied while gesturing for Apryl to shhh. "If you don't want me to do to them what you did to mine, meet me somewhere and we can do this OG style. Or are you only built to kill women and babies?"

"Ask Shaheed," he shot back.

"Fuck him, come get me, ya heard me."

"Nigga, you ain't nobody and fuck Apryl, I don't give a fuck about that ho. Go ahead and kill the ho. She ain't my woman no more no way," he said with no compassion.

"What about Asiana? "

"I don't give a fuck about nobody but myself," he responded. "But, peep this, pimp. I got somebody here with me that you care about. Hold up, I'm gon' let you holla at 'em before I run this sick dick up in her."

A moment later I heard sniffling and crying. "Prince, I'm sorry." It was my baby Nicole's voice. How had Renegade found her way down in Claxton?" I wondered, but the answer would have to wait.

"Baby, are you a'ight?" I asked. That was my only concern at the moment. Nicole didn't get a chance to respond, Renegade came back on the line.

"Nigga, you don't look for me, I look for you," he boasted. "While you was dropping money all around the city, tryna get muthafuckas to drop a dime to you about where I was at, those niggas came back and told me where I could find you. That's why I was posted up in your room when your bitch showed up. Money can't buy loyalty. I'll get back at you after I'm done running up in yo' bitch."

The line suddenly went dead.

I turned to Cap with a scowl on my face so cold it could've frozen water. "You punk muthafucka!" I gritted as my banger came up.

"Ain't no love in these streets, shawdy," he gritted as his banger came up.

Boc! Boc! Boc! Boc!

Our guns simultaneously popped off.

Ca$h

Chapter 47
Nicole

My chest heaved with fear when Renegade sat his phone down and growled, "Open up your mouth, bitch!" He had my hair wrapped around his fist.

"Please, don't do this to me," I pleaded to a man whose heart obviously held no empathy for anyone. The room was still dark. I was on my knees feeling around on the floor for my bag at the same time that I was pleading with him. Yes, I was afraid but I would rather be killed than suck him, I told myself.

Where in the hell is my bag? I fretted, not giving up quite yet.

"Bitch, you gon' make me blow your shit all over the floor. I don't give a fuck. I ain't got nothin' to lose. Now, put this dick in your mouth, and I'm not asking you again!" Renegade exploded. I had to buy time.

"Okay," I said purposely sounding as submissive as possible. I reached out and wrapped my hand around his limp penis. I slowly stroked him and felt it inflate with blood and lust.

"Yeah, get that muthafucka brick hard." He moaned. I stroked my hand up and down him like he was Prince.

"If I suck it real good, will you let me go?" I asked as I looked up into his terrifying red pupils.

"Maybe," he hoarsely replied.

I slid my hand down the length of him to his testicles and lightly rubbed them while my other hand came in contact with my Gucci bag.

"Put it in now," Renegade said as if he was speaking to a lover.

"Okay, are you ready?" I asked while taking a firm hold on the stun gun.

"Yeah—lick—the head."

I squeezed his funky nuts with all my might. "Ahhh!" he screamed. The pain had to be excruciating because he dropped his

183

gun and tried to tear my hand from around his balls, but I had them inside my closed fist and I was not letting go.

With my free hand, I pressed the stun gun on that ass. He fell to the floor. 2,900,000 volts shot from my weapon. He fell to the floor so hard I thought I had killed him because his movement had stopped. I let go of his nasty balls and snatched his gun up off the floor.

"You bastard! You're gonna pay for what you did to that woman and her child." I pointed the gun at him expecting to see him beg for his life like the coward he had to be to murder a helpless woman and child. The fucker's reaction was the exact opposite.

He finally came to his senses and mockingly laughed. "Go 'head and shoot me. Take me outta my misery. Ha! I got HIV. I'm already dying. Plus, I got the whole police department looking for me for a double homicide. You think I wanna rot away in a jail cell? Hell no! Go 'head and pull the trigger, bitch— I welcome death."

I lowered the gun. There was no way that I was giving him an easy way out. I looked at him and my mouth fired off. "Death is too good for your heartless ass. I'm gonna make you suffer."

"I'm already suffering, bitch. You can't hurt me none." I placed the stun gun on his arm and stunned that ass again. Then again…and again until he was motionless and foaming out of the mouth. I opened the curtain and let some light in. I found my cell phone in my purse. My whole body was shaking as I dialed the police.

"Please hurry…" I cried into the phone as soon as the operator answered.

"Ma'am, calm down. Can you tell me what the emergency is?" the operator asked with a pleasant tone. I guess that was her way of getting me to relax.

It all came out in a rush of emotion, and then I dropped the phone and picked the gun back up. I stood over Renegade and looked down at him, scowling. I hissed, "You killed Prince's daughter; she was the joy of his life. For that, I'm taking your life." I pulled back on the trigger.

The bullet struck just where I had intended… a few inches from his head. His body flinched. That was enough for me. He was not fearless. The only thing left was to make him suffer the wrath of the law, and live with the shame of knowing that it was a woman that had brought him to justice. I vowed to myself that I would be present the day he was put to death by lethal injection for the horrific murders of Solange and Asia.

"Open up! Police!" The pounding on the door was welcomed.

I opened the door and stepped aside as a team of officers rushed in to take Renegade into custody.

Ca$h

Chapter 48
Prince

"I wanted to kill him so bad, bae," admitted Nicole as she sat on the edge of the bed in my hospital room telling me about how frightening the ordeal had been.

"You did the right thing, hot girl. You didn't need that on your conscious, but you know I'm still hot with you for coming up here in the first place," I said trying to hold back my anger. I was just frontin' though. I was very proud of shawdy, her bravery had earned her the key to the city. She had single-handedly captured a killer who was despised by many.

"I know it was stupid of me to come up here looking for you, under the circumstances, but I was so worried," she said while looking like she had just stepped off a movie set, instead of a nightmare a day ago.

"Don't sweat it. All's well that ends well." I rubbed the side of her beautiful face as I said it.

"I'm glad you're okay." She returned my smile with a much prettier one.

I said, "Yeah, I'm good. I caught one in the stomach, but I'm blessed. I'm not in a shit bag, and I don't have a fresh murder charge, though I don't know how that nigga, Cap, lived. I popped two in that nigga's chest."

"Are they gonna charge you?"

"Na, ain't neither one of us pressing charges against the other, and Apryl isn't pressing charges either."

"Thank God!" Nicole breathed a sigh of relief.

"Now, I'm gonna get well so that I can stand at the altar with you," I said catching her off guard.

Nicole blushed, and then just as quickly a sad look came over her face. "What's wrong, baby girl?" I asked, confused.

She took a deep breath and slowly exhaled. "Prince, I have something to tell you, and I'm not sure that you'll want to marry me after you hear it." Nicole rubbed my leg then revealed to me something that I had not been prepared for. When she had explained, I said, "Nicole, it…"

"Please don't reply right away," she interrupted me. "Taka a few days to think about it. Really, I'll understand whatever you decide to do."

I picked her hand up and held it mine, and then I looked into her eyes and said, "Baby, I don't need any time to think about nothing, ya heard me. You're my *All I Need*. Nothing else matters as long as we're together." And I meant that from my heart.

Tears ran down Nicole's face in a steady stream. "I love you so much, Prince," she cried.

"And I love you, too," hot girl.

She leaned down to kiss me and I tasted her salty tears, but they were as sweet as candy.

188

Chapter 49
Epilogue

Four months later, me and Nicole exchanged wedding vows on a luxurious private resort, Casa Kimball in The Dominican Republic. The warm smooth sand was cascading across the land. There was a small breeze that offered a slight chill, which provided relief from the warm, orange-yellow setting sun. The water crashed against the rocks in the distance. Seagulls squawked overhead. Nature was in tune with the event.

Nicole's long white wedding gown clung to her body perfectly and she looked elegant. Raven stood as a maid of honor in a soft pink dress while me and Mr. Sam wore all white crisp, clean tuxedos.

Me and baby girl held hands as we waited to say our vows. A short while later, the preacher gave us the okay to begin.

Nicole began with tendrils of hair falling in her face. "Prince, I want to thank you for coming into my life and turning my pains into joy. You're my sunshine and with you I can weather any storm. On this day, I will become your wife, and I will strive to give you all of me. I'll work with you to live a wonderful life together. Your love, kindness, and gentleness inspire me to be the best person that I can be. I promise to stand by your side through your ups and downs and encourage you when you feel that the world is on your shoulders. I'm willing to face changes as we both change throughout the years. I will forever be honest, faithful, and respectful toward you as long as we both shall live, and I'll forever give you all that I am." She sniffled and a single tear of happiness trickled down her cheek. "This is my solemn vow."

I took a finger and wiped the water from Nicole's face. I held onto her hand as she whispered with a smile, "You're going to wipe away my makeup."

I smiled and shook my head. "Nicole, you're truly special, and I'm honored that you'll accept my last name. I had walls up that you slowly broke down, and you were willing to love me despite my situation. You've proven to me that no matter what, you'll ride hard for me. You diminished all of the hurt that I once felt and replaced it with your love. I'm here for you, and I always will be. Every Prince deserves a Princess, and I've found mine." Nicole's smile was so wide, and the tears were flowing like a river from the joy she was feeling. He continued, "I want to give you a lifetime of love and affection. I promise to give you all that I have to give and love you unconditionally. I will comfort you during hardships, encourage you to achieve all of your goals, and grow with you. I will always be true as long as we both live. This is my vow to you."

The preacher announced, "You may kiss the bride."

I didn't hesitate. I covered Nicole's mouth with mine and our lips remained locked for what seemed like eternity. As I kissed my beautiful bride, for that moment, all of the pain in my heart dissipated. And when I looked down in her face, I saw an expression of happiness that I promised myself I would bring time her life forever.

Baby, those that thought you were a fool for falling in love with a convict were all wrong.

The End.

Stay Connected with Us!

Text **LOCKDOWN** to 22828 to stay up-to-date with new releases, sneak peaks, contests and more…

Thank you!

Coming Soon from Lock Down Publications/Ca$h Presents

TORN BETWEEN TWO

By **Coffee**

CUM FOR ME **II**

By **Ca$h & Company**

LAY IT DOWN **III**

By **Jamaica**

BLOOD OF A BOSS **IV**

By **Askari**

BRIDE OF A HUSTLA **III**

By **Destiny Skai**

WHEN A GOOD GIRL GOES BAD **II**

By **Adrienne**

LOVE & CHASIN' PAPER **II**

By **Qay Crockett**

THE HEART OF A GANGSTA **II**

By **Jerry Jackson**

TO DIE IN VAIN **II**

By **ASAD**

THE BOSS MAN'S DAUGHTERS **II**

By **Aryanna**

Available Now

RESTRAING ORDER **I & II**

By **CA$H & Coffee**

LOVE KNOWS NO BOUNDARIES **I II & III**

By **Coffee**

LAY IT DOWN **I & II**

LAST OF A DYING BREED

By **Jamaica**

PUSH IT TO THE LIMIT

By **Bre' Hayes**

BLOOD OF A BOSS **I II & III**

By **Askari**

THE STREETS BLEED MURDER **I, II & III**

THE HEART OF A GANGSTA

By **Jerry Jackson**

CUM FOR ME

An **LDP Erotica Collaboration**

BRIDE OF A HUSTLA **I & II**

By **Destiny Skai**

WHEN A GOOD GIRL GOES BAD

By **Adrienne**

A GANGSTER'S REVENGE **I II III & IV**

THE BOSS MAN'S DAUGHTERS

A SAVAGE LOVE **I & II**

By **Aryanna**

WHAT ABOUT US **I & II**

NEVER LOVE AGAIN

THUG ADDICTION

By **Kim Kaye**

THE KING CARTEL **I, II & III**

By **Frank Gresham**

THESE NIGGAS AIN'T LOYAL **I, II & III**

By **Nikki Tee**

GANGSTA SHYT **I II &III**

By **CATO**

THE ULTIMATE BETRAYAL

By **Phoenix**

DON'T FU#K WITH MY HEART **I & II**

By **Linnea**

BOSS'N UP **I & II**

By **Royal Nicole**

I LOVE YOU TO DEATH

By **Destiny J**

<u>I RIDE FOR MY HITTA</u>
<u>I STILL RIDE FOR MY HITTA</u>
By **Misty Holt**
<u>LOVE & CHASIN' PAPER</u>
By **Qay Crockett**
<u>TO DIE IN VAIN</u>
By **ASAD**

<u>BOOKS BY LDP'S CEO, CA$H</u>

<u>TRUST IN NO MAN</u>

<u>TRUST IN NO MAN 2</u>

<u>TRUST IN NO MAN 3</u>

<u>BONDED BY BLOOD</u>

<u>SHORTY GOT A THUG</u>

<u>THUGS CRY</u>

<u>THUGS CRY 2</u>

<u>TRUST NO BITCH</u>

<u>TRUST NO BITCH 2</u>

<u>TRUST NO BITCH 3</u>

<u>TIL MY CASKET DROPS</u>

<u>RESTRAINING ORDER</u>

<u>RESTRAINING ORDER 2</u>

<u>Coming Soon</u>

THUGS CRY 3

BONDED BY BLOOD 2

BOW DOWN TO MY GANGSTA

In Love With a Convict

CPSIA information can be obtained
at www.ICGtesting.com
Printed in the USA
BVHW090220160222
629082BV00011B/900